'The Wish-List'

A novel by

Neal Hardin

ISBN 9781983329883

To my friends and colleagues in the

Central Hull Library Writers Group

(you know who you are)

Chapter 1

February 2016

You know what it's like. When you're down on your luck misfortune seems to come at you in leaps and bounds, finding the target every time. Like a first-class archer hitting the centre gold ring with every arrow. Some say that bad things come in waves of three. If ever you needed an example of that then consider, Tom Scott. Right now, he was sitting at the kitchen table in his house, with his head in his hands, nursing a sore head and wondering how his luck had ever got this bad. Who the hell had he upset to deserve this? Because, it seemed as if the entire world had it in for him.

The most recent case of bad luck concerned his one and only car. A week ago, his ten-year-old Vauxhall Corsa had given up the ghost and refused to start. He asked a friend, who just happened to be a mechanic, to come to his home to take a look. The prognosis wasn't good. A major component in the engine was faulty and needed replacing. When he received the quote for the cost of the new part and the labour it wasn't much less than the value of the car. His friend had done him a favour when he toured the car away to a scrap-yard. Now Tom needed a new vehicle.

The second case of a bad thing coming at once was the uncertainty over his job. In plain English, he didn't know if he would have one in a few weeks. Therefore, he parked the notion of buying a replacement car until he knew the situation with his job. The third item of bad news concerned his son, Josh. One month ago, Josh had

4

been sitting at a pavement table outside of a bar-café, on a street in Soho, minding his own business, and enjoying a drink with his friends. Unfortunately, for Josh a team of police officers were doing a sweep of the area, looking for drugs and to nick anyone carrying even the smallest amount of any recreational drug. Josh had been stupid enough to have a small amount of grass in his jacket pocket. A sniffer dog sniffed him out and low-and-behold he was arrested for possession of a tiny quantity of cannabis. He was fined the princely sum of five hundred pounds. As a student with hardly five hundred pence to rub together he couldn't pay the fine, so his dad had to shell out to settle his debt to society. Tom longed for a change of circumstance that would see his luck turn for the better.

It didn't turn out like that in the short term. The rumour about his job was true. The haulage distribution firm, for whom Tom worked as the depot manager, in their west London branch, were going through a sticky patch due to a sudden, unexpected downturn in demand. Consequently, Tom's job was in jeopardy. Sure, enough the firm decided to save money by closing one of their three depots in the London area. They choose the west London depot. The one Tom Scott managed. To cut a long story short he would be out of a job in the next six weeks. On the positive side he did receive the promise of a decent redundancy package, but the shock of losing his job after working continuously for the same firm for the past fifteen years came as a massive blow not only to his pocket but to his confidence and self-esteem. He would soon be out of work and out of luck.

Such was the effect of the economic downturn; some other haulage companies were going through a similar downsizing exercise. He knew that finding another job in the same line of employment and at the salary he had enjoyed could be difficult.

These three examples of bad luck had come over a six-week period, but then there was a ray of hope on the horizon. A new haulage firm based in Worcester were planning to open a new depot in a location close to Heathrow Airport. They wanted a manager. Being a native of west London Tom was more than interested in the position. He had the skills, the experience, and no pun intended, the drive. He was keen to get the job.

The salary was twenty percent less than his current job, but he wanted to work. It would get him out of a fix, until something better turned up.

After talking it over with his life partner, Riana, he completed an application form and sent it off. One week later he heard back from the firm. They wanted to interview him, so he took a trip to the lovely market town of Worcester to meet the operations manager and put his case as to why they should hire him.

Chapter 2

Tuesday 9ᵗʰ February

For the journey to and back from Worcester, Tom asked his brother-in-law, Leroy, if he could borrow his car, an old model, Mercedes C200. Leroy said okay, but he wanted it back in one piece, clean, and full of fuel.

The day of the interview was a cold, damp, and miserable Tuesday afternoon. Tom arrived at the firm's headquarters in plenty of time for the four o'clock appointment. But such was his luck he soon discovered that his interview had been put back by thirty minutes because one of the other candidates arrived late due to a pile-up on the M5. Subsequently, Tom's interview was put back to four-thirty.

When the interview finally got underway it was conducted by a lady who was the head of Human Resource and a chap who was the Director of Operations. A man who said he was a Company Director made up a panel of three. The interview lasted ten minutes short of one hour.

During the post interview reflection, Tom thought it had gone well. He had answered all their questions and supplied them with a summary of his experience, testimonials, qualifications and what-have-you. On parting, they said they would get in contact with him in a couple of days to let him know if he had been successful. So, he left the facility in Worcester at five-thirty to drive back to his home in Shepherd's Bush, west London. He hoped to be home for around seven-thirty, at the latest.

That evening, he made his way out of the town and onto the road back to London. It was a cold and wet night. There was no let-up in the rain showers that had followed him from London. He settled down to the drive back. The windscreen wipers were scraping over the windscreen. There was a stench of fumes in the back of the car and the exhaust pipe was making a God-awful rattling noise.

He had done about twenty miles along the A44 towards Oxford when the heavens opened, and the rain literally fell out of the sky with the velocity of liquid bullets. The already wet road was in some parts treacherous. Although there wasn't a lot of traffic the conditions were not the best and neither was the handling of Leroy's Merc. It was old and heavy. Driving it required a lot of care and attention. It needed four new tyres to replace the bald ones currently surfing through the spray, a tune-up to make the engine run better and a wheel balance to correct the steering mis-alignment. Rather than drive at a quick speed and run the risk of running the car off the road, he vowed not to kill himself and elected to take it easy.

He was several miles north of Oxford when he decided to pull into a lay-by to have a rest and a cigarette. His stopping in this lay-by was to prove to be one of the worst decisions of his life, or, depending on your point-of-view one of the best.

It was a long lay-by by the side of a dual-carriage section of the A44. The road ahead was on an incline as it led to the top of a hill a couple of hundred yards ahead. The glow of headlights of cars approaching the top of the hill then coming over the crest gave it a somewhat spooky halo effect as the light sprayed into the thick wooded area at both sides of the road. Though there were few cars on the road at this time of the evening it did have an eerie feel.

Tom turned off the road, drove into the lay-by, passing one parked car, then stopped about halfway along the length. He turned off the headlights, sat back and reflected for a few moments on the interview.

The more he thought about it the more pessimistic he was that he had given a good account of himself. Yes, he had the experience they required, they even acknowledged that, but he had not exactly sold himself. He had talked himself down a couple of times by admitting some minor faults. No one was perfect for God's sake. He admitted his weaknesses, when he should have glossed over them by concentrating on his strengths. It was a trait of his. On reflection, he should have sold himself more and asked them a lot more questions about the job. He should have told them what they wanted to hear, still he had answered their questions truthfully and to the best of his ability. He thought this had played well with the lady on the panel.

He reflected for a few moments, then felt inside his jacket pocket to feel for a packet of cigarettes and a lighter. He looked at his watch. The time was nearly half past six. The rain that had been battering the windscreen five minutes ago had relented and the wind blowing leaves and other debris onto the bonnet had died to a gentle breeze.

He took out the packet of cigarettes, extracted one and lit it with the lighter, then he remembered that he was in Leroy's car. His brother-in-law had asked him not to smoke in his car. Not wishing to upset him Tom opened the door, got out of the driver's seat, stepped around the front and onto the path.

An over-full concrete rubbish bin was spewing litter onto the path. The damp stench of the earth in the wooded area beyond the path and the short wooden fence to the side filled his nostrils. He looked up the lay-by to where another car was parked around thirty yards away. The lights were out. He glanced back to the first car which was about twenty yards behind him. Its lights were also out. Tom assumed that both drivers - were like him - taking a rest or even a nap. Up ahead on the crest of the hill the full beam headlights of a car appeared to illuminate the crest of the hill, then the vehicle came over the summit and down the descent at a fair speed.

He sucked on the cigarette and savoured the taste of the tobacco at the back of his throat. He would have this smoke, then get on his way. If he kept the pedal to the metal for the next thirty miles he would soon be on the M40, then onto the A40 for the run into west London. The first thing he was going to do when he got home was to make a cup of tea and have a sandwich or something that didn't take long to prepare.

With that he took in a couple of deep pulls on the cigarette and let the fumes fill his lungs. Such was the deep intake that it made him cough. He cleared his throat then threw the burning cigarette to the ground. He was about to stamp it out when he heard the sound of a crack coming out of the wooded area.

He looked into the cover of the trees, but it was pitch black in there. All he could see was the thick cover of trees and bush. Although he couldn't be certain the noise he had heard sounded like the crack of a gunshot. He asked himself who the hell would be shooting a gun in a pitch-black wood miles from anywhere? Then he thought it must have been a farmer in the surrounding fields or one of those machines that emit a loud clap to scare crows and what-have-you. He didn't think a lot more about it and moved a couple of feet to move around to the driver's door, then it happened again. Another crack. A similar sound to the first one. About fifteen seconds after the first one.

This time the sound was if anything a lot sharper and nearer to him than the first. He looked up towards the parked car. Maybe, the driver had heard the sound. Perhaps he should go and ask, but maybe not. Maybe the best course of action was to get going? As he was about to go around the front of his car he heard another sound. It was the sound of something or someone trampling through the wooded area. It was so spooky it frightened him, but he stayed still and peered into the trees as best as he could. He could clearly hear someone or an animal moving through the undergrowth. Maybe it was a deer or some other animal. There had been a sign a couple of miles back warning about deer in this area. Maybe it was a deer, and someone was shooting at it in some kind of a night hunt.

Tom was somewhat apprehensive and moved around to get behind the car should a fully-grown deer come tearing out of the trees. There was no vision to be had so he stepped up onto the pavement and continued to peer into the wood. There was nothing to see except for tall spindly trees, thick bush and undergrowth, but then a human figure appeared at the cusp of the opening into the wood.

"Who is it?" Tom shouted. Whoever it was didn't reply. Then in the next moment a figure emerged through a gap in the fence and came into the open. Tom peered at the figure. "Who is it?" he asked again nervously. Again, there was no response. The figure appeared to be bent over at the waist and struggling to stay upright. The figure was wearing dark clothing. He or she had a cap or a hat of some description on their head.

The figure emerged from out of the grassy area, stepped over a narrow grass verge and onto the path, just a matter of ten yards or so from Tom. It looked like a man who was wearing a dark waist length jacket that reflected the light. He had dark trousers and a dark peaked cap on his head. He was carrying a bag or an item of luggage in his hand.

"Who is it?" Tom asked for the third time. The person heard him, raised his head, and looked in his direction. Whoever it was, was struggling to move in a straight line. He appeared to be staggering as if he was drunk. This was so bizarre. Tom wondered what on earth was going on. Despite feeling apprehensive and a little pensive he decided to stay with it. The man may have been hurt.

The figure came towards him in a slow, robotic like step. He was soon at the corner of the car. It was then that Tom saw the splash of red at the man's lower abdomen. He didn't know what it was for sure until the man was standing next to the front passenger door of the Mercedes. The red was blood and there was a great deal of it. The figure was now panting as if the task of walking out of the wood had taken a great deal of effort and all his energy was being sucked out of his body. Tom was stunned.

"You okay?" he asked. The figure gargled out a couple of words which were undecipherable, then he almost stumbled and fell into Tom. He was wearing a black leather zip-up jacket which had a hole in it, the size of a clenched fist, where a hole shouldn't have been. He had a black woolly peaked cap on his head. In his gloved hand he held a sports bag which looked heavy. His grip was tight.

Tom was now half trembling, half with fear and half with the cold. The red of the man's blood covered the lower half on his stomach area. It was glistening in the moonlight.

"What the fuck happened to you?" Tom asked.

The man was a white guy. From what Tom could tell he was around thirty to forty years of age. He looked at Tom. With a combination of sweat and raindrops his face had a waxy pallor tint. There was a glazed look in his eyes. That look of total and absolute confusion.

"I've …been shot," he said in a whispered mutter.

"Shot?" Tom exclaimed. "By who?" he asked. The man didn't reply. "Are you okay?"

"Far from it," said the man. "Get me to a hospital. I'm bleeding to death," he said.

"All right. Yeah. Good idea." Was all that Tom could say. He was totally dumfounded. Almost too stunned for words of his own. Nevertheless, he acted decisively. He went around the front of the car, opened the driver's door and got into the car, then reaching across he opened the passenger door.

"Get in," he encouraged.

The fellow managed to open the door wide and climb into the car. He plumped into the seat, then let out a groan. *Fuck sake,* thought Tom. He needed this like he needed a hole in his head. He was in the car with someone he didn't know from a hole in the ground who had a gunshot wound to his stomach which was spewing blood like no one's business. Then he realised it wasn't his car. What the hell would Leroy say if he found blood all over the front passenger seat? He would be less than pleased, to put it mildly.

"Where's the nearest hospital?" Tom asked. "Do you know?"

The man looked at him with a kind of stupefied, drunk look on his face. He didn't say a word. He seemed more concerned with keeping the contents of the sports bag close to him. His arms were tightly clamped around it as if it contained all his worldly possessions.

Tom started the engine, edged the car along the lay-by, went passed the other parked vehicle and drove out onto the A44.

Tom didn't hang about. He gave it full throttle. The last thing he needed was this man passing away in a car he had no insurance for. The police would ask questions and he would get himself into a heap of trouble.

After a couple of hundred yards he came to a road sign indicating a turn off to a place called 'Yanton'. Oxford was only a couple of miles away further along the road.

On hitting the outskirts of Oxford, Tom came to a roundabout onto the A40 and there was the sign he had been hoping to see. A white letter H on red background. The sign for a nearby hospital. The John Radcliffe hospital was close by. If he could get this guy into the A&E department there was a good chance that he wouldn't expire in the passenger seat. The man's head suddenly slumped forward, and he seemed to be making these odd wheezing sounds. It was almost possible to hear the squelch of blood coming out of his abdomen. There was an aroma in the car Tom had never smelt before. Maybe it was the smell of death.

"You okay? Hang on," he encouraged. "There's an hospital near to here," he said. "Please, don't die on me," he pleaded.

Within the next couple of hundred yards the six-storey building of the main section of the John Radcliffe hospital came into view. Lights were blazing in most of the upper level windows. An ambulance with its emergency blue, red and white lights flashing and siren blasting out was just ahead. As he had no idea where the A&E department was located Tom followed it around a roundabout then along a road running by the side of a long building for several hundred yards, before it turned into a forecourt in front of a wide glass sliding door under a canopy. The words: 'Accident and Emergency department', were displayed in big, bold letters.

He drove up to the doors. Questions about how he had found this man filled his mind, but still he knew his priority was to get this fellow, whoever he was, into the unit. He would try to answer any questions when they were put to him.

He managed to pull up as near as possible to the wide glass sliding doors leading into the A&E unit. Then he got out of the car, went around to the passenger side and opened the door. He took hold of the chap and managed to wrestle him out. He looked around for help, but no one was near him.

After a bit of a tussle he managed to lift the guy out of the passenger seat and get him to his feet. The sports bag, with whatever it contained, fell into the foot-well. The fellow grunted something, but his words didn't make any sense. He appeared to be in a semi-comatose like state. No doubt the loss of so much blood had lowered his blood pressure which had put him into a kind of shock.

Even though the chap was quite a weight and bulky around the upper body, Tom managed to put his left arm under his shoulder and drag him towards the sliding door. Just then the sliding door opened and a man, wearing a blue nurse's uniform came outside and stood just outside the door.

"Help," shouted Tom.

The chap looked up. He didn't expect to be greeted by the sight of the two men. One dragging the other who was clearly losing a lot of blood from an open wound to his stomach.

"Wait there," the man shouted. "I'll get a trolley."

The chap hot-foot it back inside the door. He emerged less than fifteen seconds later with two hospital porters close to him and a stretcher on wheels. Between all four of them they got the injured man onto the stretcher and pushed it through the doors and inside the A&E unit.

Tom was about to follow the three hospital personnel inside the door. Then something made him pause. He suddenly thought what the hell. He didn't know the victim and the victim didn't know him. He didn't know how he had sustained the injury to his stomach. It was nothing to do with him. The smart move might be to get away from here, while he could. Someone entering a hospital with a man who had a serious looking injury, which was in all likelihood inflicted by a shotgun was bound to be asked a lot of questions. Tom didn't want to be detained and asked a lot of questions for which he didn't have any answers.

He glanced back to the Mercedes. Leroy wanted it back tomorrow morning. Then he felt the keys in his hand and thought here was his chance to get away before the police arrived and he was detained for the next ten hours to answer the Why's, the When's, and the What's.

With those thoughts percolating through his head he looked to the glass sliding doors which were just about to close. He stopped

17

dead in his tracks, turned one hundred and eighty degrees and briskly walked across the forecourt, got into the Mercedes, closed the door, started the engine, and drove out of the hospital grounds.

From here he drove through Oxford, found a road that led onto the M40 and drove onto the motorway. Once he was on the motorway it was only a relatively short distance of around thirty-five miles to his home on Goldhawk Road in west London.

First thing, the following morning, he would clean the car from top to bottom and get rid of the blood. Leroy was coming to collect the car at ten o'clock.

Chapter 3

It was approaching twenty past nine when Tom arrived home at the house he shared with his partner Riana. The house was in a typical row of nineteen-fifties houses on a suburban road off Goldhawk Road. Shepherd's Bush Green was a five-minute walk away. It was an area Tom knew well from his childhood. The house he lived in was his late parents' home when he was a kid growing up. Sadly, his parents had died within two years of each other when he was in his late twenties. He missed them terribly, but at least they had bequeathed the house to him, their only child.

He parked the Merc on the hard-standing in front of the window. A light was shining in the lounge. He didn't know what he was going to say to Riana. Her half-brother, Leroy Panther, was his best mate from way back when. They had known each other since they played football together for a Sunday league team from Hounslow. Riana was Leroy's half-sister. Leroy had introduced Tom to Raina. They hit it off immediately and one thing led to another. That was eight years ago.

He killed the engine, waited for a moment to get his thoughts together, then he got out of the car and entered the house. Riana was there to greet him. She was the love of his life. She had a dusky Caribbean complexion. Dark brown eyes. Curly corkscrew hair that she had dyed a copper-red shade, a nice face, and an ample figure. Not obese, but ample.

As he stepped into the house she immediately clapped her eyes on the smudge of blood on his jacket. Her puzzled concerned look told him she had seen something untoward before he could utter a word of explanation.

"Oh, my God. What's that?" she asked with a startled tone in her voice and a mixture of horror and concern on her face.

"Long story," he said as he wriggled out of the jacket without getting blood on his hands or on his shirt. She could see by his still white shirt that it wasn't his blood.

"Is that what I think it is?" she asked.

"If you think its blood. Then you're not wrong," he said. He had concocted a story about how he had hit a deer on the A40. How he had got out of the car to move the animal off the road and in doing so got blood on him. But maybe that was too farfetched. She knew he would never have got out of the car to attend to a dying animal.

"What happened?" she asked.

"You wouldn't believe me if I told you."

"Care to try me?" she asked.

He stepped into the front room, the lounge, and aimed for the sofa. The room was quaint. Riana had a penchant for interior design and a gift for creating rich fabric coverings in a colourful Caribbean colour scheme. The furniture and decoration were simple yet eminently tasteful and full of green, yellow, and red. He did think the whole house was over cluttered with an assortment of nick-knacks and souvenirs Riana had collected on her numerous trips to the Caribbean. An oil painting of the late, great Robert Nesta Marley took pride of place over the mantelpiece above the fireplace, alongside a framed poster of the late, John Lennon posing in a New York City t-shirt. Riana was talking about replacing it with a picture of Usain Bolt, though Tom much preferred deceased music icons over sport stars. He said they had more creditability, though how he came to that conclusion he wasn't sure.

He plumped into the centre of the sofa, Riana sat in an armchair. The TV was on, but the volume had been muted.

"Are you going to tell me?" she asked peevishly.

"Yeah. I suppose I'd better," he said.

He told her everything. How he had been driving along the A44 towards Oxford. How he had stopped in the lay-by for a cigarette. The sound of the gunshots, or what he assumed were gunshots. Then how the figure had come scrambling out of the undergrowth and approached him. How he saw the hole in his jacket and the blood. How he had taken him to the Accident and Emergency unit in the John Radcliffe Hospital in Oxford and how he had backed away and decided to get away before the police arrived and asked him a barrage of questions.

She took it all in and considered several theories that were percolating in her head. Then she began by asking the obvious question.

"Whose were the two cars parked in the lay-by?" she asked.

"I've no idea. Maybe one was his. Not sure whose the other belonged to. There didn't seem to be anyone in the cars."

"What about the two gunshots?"

"What about them?" he asked.

"Did he fire one?" Riana asked.

"Who?"

"Who do you think? The man you took to the hospital."

"I suppose he could have."

"If there were two shots did he do one? Maybe he shot the other one."

"Maybe. Maybe the one who shot him fired both the shots. I've no way of knowing."

"Yeah. I see what you mean," she said. "How long apart were the shots?"

"A few seconds."

"How many?" Riana asked.

"Five. Ten. I'm not so sure," he replied.

Riana considered his answers and seemed to be creating a possible scenario in her head. "Maybe there were two people in the wood," she said. "They were meeting there. After all there were two cars parked in the lay-by. They had some kind of argument."

"About what?" he asked.

"Who knows. They had a disagreement about something. Shots were fired. They shoot each other. Your guy gets hit, but he's able to get out of the wood and return to his car. Maybe the other one ran away," she said. She seemed to be enjoying the intrigue of what might have happened. To be honest he could do without it.

"Or maybe he's lying in there right now, having been shot," Tom said.

"Yeah. I suppose it's possible."

"We're guessing what it might have been about."

"Maybe there was only one guy there. Maybe the gun went off by accident and he shot himself. It's possible," she said.

"I dare say it's possible. But the truth is we're pissing in the wind." Tom said and sighed aloud. He felt fatigued and confused.

Riana made a loud *hmmh*. "Was he carrying anything?" she asked.

"Who?"

"The man who got into the car."

"Shit!" Tom exclaimed.

"What?"

"He was carrying a big sports bag."

"Where is it?" she asked.

"It's in the car," replied Tom. He jumped up off the sofa. He had forgotten all about the sports bag which was in the foot-well at the passenger side. "I'll go and get it," he said.

He went outside to the Mercedes, opened the driver's side, reached across over the passenger seat and sure enough the sports bag was still lodged tightly into the foot space. He grasped hold of it and tried to pull it out, but it was surprising heavy and awkward to get free. He had to use both hands to lift it and pull it out. It was that heavy.

Maybe ten kilos or so, at a guess. On first feel it appeared to be full of similar shape bundles of paper.

He quickly took it inside the house, locked the front door, stepped into the front room, and put it down on the rug in front of the fireplace. It was a cigar shaped sports bag. The kind of thing you'd see on any high-street. The motif of a well-known sports brand was displayed in bold white letters on the black surface.

Riana looked at it. "What's inside?" she asked.

"No idea," he replied.

He took the zip tag and pulled it open. What was inside the bag caused them both to look at each other and say, "Fucking hell' simultaneously. Inside the bag there were bundles of used banknotes, stacked into tightly packed wads of cash. There were fifty-pound notes, twenties, ten and fives. A lot of them. All secured by thin rubber elastic bands.

The smell of used banknotes was almost overpowering. The shades of the purples, oranges and the greens were like a paint colour chart.

"Oh my God," he said. He looked at Riana. She looked at him and they could only share a stunned, wide-eyed expression. "It's full of cash," he said.

"How much?" she asked.

He looked at her. "How the hell do I know?" he snapped.

He ran a hand across his mouth. The reality of the moment was dawning on him. The bag was full to bursting with cash. A lot of cold hard cash. The bag was deep. He dipped his hand inside and weaved to the bottom. It was all cash. There was nothing else inside. There was a zipped pocket at each end. He opened them, one at a time, and pulled out various documents. There was an EU UK passport. A ticket of some description and a receipt from a sports shop in Oxford for the purchase of a sports bag.

He opened the passport at the back page and looked at the photograph of the holder. He couldn't recognise the photo as the face of the man he had taken to the hospital. The man in the photo had a shaved head. The man in the car had been wearing a woolly peak cap, maybe it was the same man. Maybe it wasn't. The passport gave the name of the man as: Lyle Anton Kemp. Aged forty-five-years-of-age. Birthplace London. The pages were full of border stamps, suggesting that the holder was a frequent traveller. There were stamps from the United States, Canada, Hong Kong, Australia, as well as countries throughout South America. He passed the passport to Riana.

"Look at this. He's well-travelled," he said. She took it but didn't open the pages. Her eyes were on the stacks of banknotes.

"How much is there?" she asked again.

He refrained from snapping at her a second time. "No idea," he said, then he gave her a kind of reflective, serious look. "I've no idea. I suppose we'd better count it."

Riana slid off the armchair and joined him on her knees on the floor. He began to extract the wads of cash out of the bag and stack them on the carpet.

"That's the first thing we need," she said.

"What's that?" he asked.

"A new carpet."

He said nothing. He continued to take the bundles out and arrange them into a neat pile on the floor. The time by the carriage clock on top of the mantel piece said nine-thirty-two. A few minutes passed before all the bundles of cash were out of the bag. They were neatly stacked. He arranged them into a grid consisting of two rows, four columns in each. By the time all the bundles were out the pile was six high. A total of forty-eight bundles of used Bank of England notes.

"Get a pen and a piece of blank paper will you," Tom asked.

"Why?" she asked.

"We need to begin a shopping list."

She chuckled. "You serious?"

"I'm kidding. We need to add up how much is here," he said raising his voice ever so slightly.

"How much would you say?" she asked as if it was some kind of a guessing game.

He looked at her. "I'll take a wild stab in the dark. I'll guess four hundred thousand." As he said that it finally dawned on him. This incongruous sight of so many banknotes would add up to be a pretty substantial sum of money.

Riana got to her feet. She went into the kitchen and came back moments later with a cheap biro and a piece of notepad paper she used for writing messages and her shopping list.

He took the first wad of cash, peeled the rubber band off and began to count the value of the notes. It needed a couple of attempts to count it, after all he wasn't used to counting this amount of cash, plus his train of thought was finding it difficult to concentrate on the task.

After several minutes of counting the first wad came to exactly £8,320.

By the time the clock chimed midnight they had counted twenty-six of the forty-eight bundles. The running aggregate total to midnight was £278,550.

At one o'clock in the morning, they took a ten-minute break and went into the back garden for a cigarette and a drink of coffee. The morning air was sharp but laced with a hint of a warm southerly breeze which meant it wasn't that chilly.

After the break, they returned to the task. A further two hours passed. As the clock hit three-twenty they had completed the task. Each one of the forty-eight bundles had been counted and the sum of each had been recorded. Of course, there was no guarantee that it was accurate.

Rather than doing mental arithmetic to provide a final total Tom turned on his home PC, Riana read out the figures and he fed them into a spreadsheet. Despite steadily growing fatigue they managed to complete the task. The total of all forty-eight bundles, give or take a couple of grand either way was a whooping £571,870.

Rather than leave the cash littering the lounge floor Tom put the bundles back into the sports bag, zipped it closed, then he took the bag upstairs to their bedroom and placed it under a pile of blankets in a blanket box.

Before going to bed Tom ensured that the front and back doors were locked and secure, and all the lights were turned off.

"What are we going to do with it?" Riana asked.

"No idea," replied Tom as he climbed into bed and snuggled up to her.

He lay there. His head deep into the pillow, looking up at the ceiling, thinking. He had no idea what they were going to do with the cash. The questions that came back to him repeatedly were: *Whose cash is it?* and *Where did it come from?* He had no answer to both questions. The idea of keeping it and starting a new life in Trinidad was one that crossed his mind. It was something they had talked about. Like a wish-list of desires and aspirations that they would never achieve. Riana's family originated from that island. She had often talked about going there to start a new life. It was a pipe dream. One item on her substantial wish-list was to be out of the grime of London and onto a beautiful Caribbean island. Now it just might become a reality.

Before getting carried away with planning a new life, first, Tom had to clean the car and give it to Riana's half-brother. Maybe they should tell Leroy. Maybe they shouldn't. Maybe it would only be a matter of time before the police came knocking at his door.

Neither of them slept much that morning. It was six-thirty when Tom got out of bed. The inbuilt alarm clock in his body didn't allow him to sleep in, though he wasn't going to work anymore. He had been getting up at six-thirty a.m. every day for the past eight years, even on weekends, therefore he was an early riser. He couldn't sleep anyway.

During what sleep he had got he had a dream in which he had seen the waxy face of a man disappearing underwater. He had been mouthing words he couldn't hear clearly enough to decipher. Then he was gone under the water and never came back. It was a dream that had left him with a sheet of cold perspiration on his body.

He slipped into his clothing without disturbing Riana, who was sleeping like a baby. Before he went downstairs he looked into the blanket box to make sure he had not dreamt the entire episode. It was no dream. The sports bag full of cash was real all right. He could smell that scent of used banknotes.

Once dressed he went downstairs into the kitchen, made himself a slice of toast and a mug of strong black coffee. Then he sat at the kitchen table. At a time approaching seven, he collected a spray bottle of cleaning liquid, a chamois leather, a cloth and went outside to the car on the hard-standing. The weak watery sunlight of morning was coming over the city. The thin patch of frost on the street wouldn't last long. As soon as the sun got out it would be gone. There was some movement on the street with neighbours beginning to emerge out of their homes to make their way to their place of work or wherever they were going.

The sound of the traffic on Goldhawk Road was already beginning to make itself heard. One thing never changed from one day to the next and that was the familiar sound of the rush hour. One thing he wouldn't miss if he ever left London, was the madness of the city and the crippling pace of life.

Chapter 4

Wednesday 10th February

Tom sprayed a soapy cleaning liquid onto the passenger seat and attempted to wipe the blood off the seat and the rubber mats on the floor. There was even a smudge on the gear stick and the dashboard, so he ran the cloth over the surface. He ended up cleaning the entire inside of the car. To complete the job, he cleaned the bodywork with a bucket of soapy water and a sponge. One hour after leaving the house he returned to the kitchen. Riana was sitting at the table in her fluffy robe nursing a cup of coffee.

She eyed him but didn't say anything and neither did he. He put the cleaning materials back into the cupboard below the sink, then he sat at the table opposite Riana and just relaxed as best as he could.

"Was there a lot?" she asked glumly.

"A lot of what?"

"Blood."

"Enough."

"What are you going to say to Leroy? If he notices," she asked.

"I don't think he'll notice. The car is hardly new inside. There's already a huge stain on the seat. He might not notice," he replied.

There were a few moments of silence, whilst they contemplated things going forward. The toaster popped two slices of toast and the fragrance of burnt bread filled the kitchen.

Riana got up from the table and did the honours. She put a slice of butter smeared toast on a plate and placed it in front of him. She had the other slice.

"I wonder if the man survived?" she asked as though it was an afterthought.

"So, do I. I guess we'll find out soon enough," he replied.

"What do you mean?" she asked.

He took a bite of the toast and chewed on it then swallowed hard. He looked at her. "We'll have to keep watching the news. It may be only a matter of time before the police start...."

"A matter of time to what?"

"Until the police ask for assistance. They may get in touch with Leroy."

"How?" she asked.

"CCTV. They'll have the car on the cameras in the hospital grounds. Unless the cameras were off, which I doubt. The police will be able to trace the car to your brother by the registration number."

Riana sat up. "In that case. I think we'd better tell him to expect a call from the police," she said.

He contemplated her suggestion for a few brief moments, then nodded his head. "I think you're right," he said.

"Do we tell him about finding the money?" she asked.

"That's a good question. Not sure. But we'd better get our story straight."

"What story?"

"How I came to be at a hospital Accident and Emergency department delivering a dying man to them."

"Then how you took fright and left before giving your name."

"Yeah. That's right."

"Perhaps you ought to call the police," she said.

"Perhaps I ought to. But tell them what exactly?"

"How you stopped in the lay-by for a cig. How you heard two gunshots. How the man with the wound came out of the wood. How you drove him to the hospital…"

He considered her words. "Yeah. How I panicked, because it wasn't my car."

"Then how you saw that the man was being attended to and didn't want to get involved."

Tom's face became one of concern and thought. "Geez. There could be someone else dead in that wood. This could get tricky. I might be done for leaving the scene of a crime."

"You panicked because it wasn't your car. You've got no insurance to drive that car. They won't do you for that."

"You think?"

"They'll understand," she said. "The only thing you don't say is that the man had a sports bag full of money with him. It would be your word against his."

"What if he died?"

"Then it's your word against no ones." Riana was being incredibly pragmatic. As if she had thought this through in a rational manner and considered every possibility.

Tom raised his head and looked at her. "Your right," he said. "I think we'd better hide that bag somewhere. Think of a place to put it."

"How about the loft?" she said.

"Too obvious."

"Under the bath."

"No"

"Errr…"

"Let's leave it up there for now. I'm more concerned about what I tell Leroy," said Tom.

Riana looked at the clock on the wall. The time was now getting on for nine o'clock. "He's coming here in an hour," she said.

"I know. Let's put the TV on. See if there's a report on the news about someone suffering from a gunshot wound being taken to a hospital in Oxford."

They went into the front room. He put the TV on and they sat on the sofa together to watch the rolling news on the Sky TV News channel.

In the forty-five minutes from nine to nine forty-five there was no mention of a gunshot victim being taken into John Radcliffe hospital last night. They could relax for the moment. At ten-to-ten

Tom received a text on his mobile phone. It was from Leroy to inform him that he was coming around in ten minutes to collect his car.

Leroy Panther arrived at Tom and Riana's home right on the hour of ten. He was punctual. If he said he was going to be there at a certain time, then he would be there – come hell or high water.

Riana and Leroy looked like brother and sister, but there was one subtle difference. They shared the same mother, but not the same father. Leroy's dad was a white guy called Ronnie Panther, whereas Riana's father was a light skinned Caribbean guy called Lucas Thomas. Ronnie Panther and Tony Scott – Tom's dad had worked for the same engineering firm in Ealing. They had become good friends. That is how Tom and Leroy had met. They knew each other from their earliest schooldays and even played in the same football and cricket teams up until their mid-twenties.

Leroy was a stout, thick bodied guy who occasionally worked out in a local gym. At six-two he had excelled as a football player and an all-round cricketer. He had trials with Surrey Cricket Club in his youth and very nearly made the grade as a county cricketer. Brentford Football club had given him a non-professional contract at the age of sixteen, but he failed to make it to the professional grade, though he did turn out for a couple of semi-professional teams in the west London area until a knee injury put an end to that. Now he worked as an electrical engineer for British Telecom in west London.

With dark eyes and his mother's features mixed in with his dad's good looks he was a very handsome guy who had many female admirers. The only woman to melt his heart was the woman he had met ten years ago. She was an Aussie called Marie Slater. They had met by chance at a cricket club event and had hit it off instantly and quickly became an item. They shared a love nest in nearby Acton.

Ironically, perhaps, though Leroy and Riana shared the same mother they weren't that close. A family dispute, that Riana rarely spoke about, seemed to be the catalyst to a relationship that was at times strained. Tom never interrogated Riana about the dispute. It was little to do with him. He had enough of his own woes with his son Josh who tended to go off the rails every now and again.

Leroy came into the house. He was dressed casually in jeans, a plain looking sweatshirt, and a red Ferrari logo baseball cap on his head.

He greeted his half-sister with a pleasant 'hello'. She responded in the same manner. He looked at Tom. "How did the interview go?" he asked.

"Okay," was Tom's somewhat downbeat response.

"Only okay?"

"Nothing special."

"When do they let you know?"

"Oh. You know, the usual bullshit. They've got hundreds of people to interview. They'll let me know as soon as they reach a decision. Could be a few days. Could be a week. They didn't exactly give me a time."

"Confident?"

"Of what?"

"Signing for Chelsea. What'd think? Getting the job."

"Yeah. But that doesn't always mean much. Does it?"

"For God's sake. Lighten up. You might get it," said Leroy.

"Yeah. That's true."

"I see you've put the car through a car wash. Either that or you've given it a wash."

"The latter."

"Hark at you. The latter," Leroy laughed. "How did it perform?"

"All right. Thanks."

"Needs four new tyres. And a balance."

"Tell me about it," said Tom under his breath.

"Got the keys?"

Tom looked at him with a serious face. "I think you'd better take a seat."

Leroy gave him a puzzled type of face as if Tom had just asked him a tricky general knowledge question. "Why? Is the engine fucked?" he asked.

"Nothing like that, but I think you'd better take a seat."

Leroy retained the puzzled expression. He pulled a seat from under the table and sat down. "What is it?" he asked.

"The police might be getting in touch with you."

"Why?"

"Last night. Coming home on the A44. I pulled into a lay-by just on the other side of Oxford. A place called Yanton. For a smoke."

"Yeah I know it. So?"

"You won't believe this…"

"Try me."

"I got out of the car because I know you'd go nuts if I smoked in the car.…"

"Too right."

"Be serious for a moment."

"Okay."

"I heard two gunshots."

Leroy's jaw dropped open to reveal the bottom row of his teeth. "What? Two *gunshots*?"

"Yeah. In the woods. Next thing this bloke comes staggering out of the wood. He's been shot in the stomach." Tom touched his lower abdomen to show him the location.

"You're kidding?" Leroy asked, stunned and bemused.

"No, I wish I was."

"And?"

"I put the bloke in your car and drove him to the hospital."

"Just like anyone would."

"Listen. I panicked."

"What'd mean I panicked? You saw he was okay. Didn't you?"

"Yeah, of course, but I left the hospital without giving a name or speaking to anyone."

"Why?"

"I panicked. I don't have insurance to drive your car," Tom said.

"Of course, you don't. Why would you?"

"I drove to the Accident and Emergency unit and got him out the car and was carrying him inside when these blokes in porter's outfits appeared. They took him inside. I was going to go in but cleared off."

"So?"

"So, the police are going to want to speak to the guy who drove him to the hospital."

"That's you," said Leroy.

"Yeah. I know that, but you're the registered owner of the car. If the hospital give the police the CCTV they'll trace the car to you. Won't they…?"

Leroy put his hand to his chin and rubbed it. The penny had dropped. "Yeah. Of course. I'm the registered keeper."

"That's right."

"Oh my God…" Leroy drummed his fingers against his chin. "There was something on LBC this morning about a bloke who'd been shot, and he'd been taken to a hospital in Oxford last night. Is it the same one?"

"What time was that?" Riana asked.

"About half-seven this morning. Is it the same one?" Leroy asked again.

"Probably. Oxford is hardly like the south-side of Chicago is it?" said Tom.

Leroy opened his hands wide. "Why don't you call the police in Oxford? Tell them what happened. They're bound to understand why you legged it, but you should report what you heard and what happened. If the police, contact me. I can't tell them jack shit. They'll want to know who was using the car. I can't say the invisible man. Can I?"

"No. Of course not," said Tom.

He looked at Riana who offered him a neutral face. Leroy had effectively backed him into a corner with no way out.

"When you heard about the shooting on LBC. Did they say if the guy was dead?" Tom asked.

"To tell you the truth I wasn't listening that closely. Have a look on-line?"

"Good idea," said Riana.

She got up from the table and led them into a small room they used as a study. It was nothing special. Just a table that housed a cheap PC, a printer, some other electrical equipment, their collection of DVD's and what-not. Riana turned on the PC and sat in the black leather office chair.

Tom and Leroy remained standing at her side, looking over her shoulder. She pulled up Google and typed, 'Oxfordshire Police' into the search engine. The search engine directed her to the Thames Valley Police web-site. There under the navigation top line was the following banner headline:

Shot man, 46, dies in John Radcliffe Hospital, overnight.

Riana pulled open the report under the heading: >For more information

She read the text of the report out loud:

This morning, a so far unnamed man has died after been taken to the Accident and Emergency department of the John Radcliffe Hospital, at seven o'clock last night. The man, who had a severe, gunshot wound to the abdomen was taken to the hospital by an unknown person. Police are seeking to trace the owner of a Mercedes motor car that left the hospital soon after the man had been admitted. This remains a live investigation and we continue to appeal for the public's help. If you have any

information about this incident,
please call Thames Valley police
in the central Oxford station and
quote reference number 6705.

There was a telephone number to call. Riana finished reading the text, pushed herself back and put her hands behind her head.

"That's what you've got to do," said Leroy, looking at Tom. "Call the police and get yourself off the hook."

"I heard you," said Tom. He took a pencil off the desk, a piece of note paper and wrote the telephone number on it. Then he took his mobile phone, tapped in the telephone number, and put it on loud loudspeaker. He felt a weight lifting from off his shoulders.

His call was answered as the fourth ring ended and the fifth was beginning. The receiver introduced herself. "Thames Valley police. How may I help you?" she asked.

"Can I speak to someone about the man who died from the gunshot wound in Radcliffe Hospital this morning?" Tom asked.

"Tell him the reference," said Riana in low voice.

"Can I take your name please?" the operator asked.

"Thomas Scott."

"Mister Scott. I'll transfer you to the incident room," she said.

"Thank you."

The line went dead momentarily as the call was transferred, then the telephone was picked up and the person on the other end of the line introduced himself:

"Detective Chief Inspector Derek Goodall. How can I help you?" asked the voice.

"It's about the man who died this morning from the gunshot wound. I have some information."

"Do you know his name?" the detective asked.

"Lyle Kemp," he replied.

"How do you know that?"

Shit! thought Tom. His first serious mistake. He sought to rectify it. "He told me," he said.

"When did he tell you?"

"Last night."

"What's your full name?"

"Thomas Norman Scott." Leroy nearly let out a snigger. Tom seldom used his middle name. He hated it with a passion.

"When did you meet with Mister Kemp?"

"Last night."

"How?" DCI Goodall asked.

"I was driving along the A44 last night. I was around five miles or so from Oxford. I stopped in a lay-by for a nap and a cigarette."

"Were you driving an old type of C200 Mercedes?"

"Yes. How do you know that?"

"What's the registration?"

43

One moment. Tom looked to Leroy. "What's the registration?" he asked.

"LK03 7TY," said Leroy.

Tom repeated it to the detective on the other end of the line.

"Did you take the victim to the John Radcliffe hospital?" he asked.

"Yes. I did."

"Why didn't you stay with the victim?" the cop asked.

"I didn't know him," said Tom. "It was nothing to do with me. I did my bit by taking him to the hospital. I don't know why he was shot or who shot him. I guess I panicked and wanted to get away."

Goodall didn't reply for a few moments. Maybe he was musing over his words. There was a tiny sound of a click on the line as if someone else had picked up a receiver to listen in on the conversation or maybe it was a recording device being activated.

"That's understandable," he said. "What time was it when you stopped in the lay-by?"

"Not sure, about half six to quarter to seven. I'd been for a job interview in Worcester. I didn't get out of the depot until about five-thirty, then I hit the rain and had to slow right down. I didn't get to the lay-by until about that time."

"What happened in the lay-by?" Goodall asked.

"I got out of the car. I was dying for a smoke and a breath of fresh air. Then I heard two shots."

"Two gunshots?" the detective asked.

"Yeah. Gunshots."

"Did they come together instantly?"

"No. I'd say there was a ten second gap between them. Next thing I hear is someone coming through the bush and the bracken. Then he comes out and steps onto the path by the lay-by…"

"You sure you heard two separate shots? Are you certain?" Goodall asked.

"Positive."

"Could one have been an echo of the first?"

"I doubt it."

"Why?"

"They were too far apart and sounded different."

"Okay. Then what?" Goodall asked.

"The guy was staggering. I thought he was pissed. But as he got nearer I could see he was bleeding heavily from a wound to his stomach. There was blood everywhere."

"Then what?"

"I asked him if he was okay."

"What did he say?" Goodall asked.

"Nothing much."

"But he told you his name?" the cop asked in a dual question, statement of fact.

"That was in the car."

"Okay. Carry on."

"I could see that he was badly hurt so I managed to get him into the passenger seat. As I was only a few miles from Oxford, I

45

thought there must be a hospital not too far away. I drove into the town."

"How was the victim?" Goodall asked.

"In the car?" Tom asked.

"Yes. Did he talk much?"

"He didn't say a lot. I asked him for his name. He said Lyle Kemp."

"You sure it's Lyle Kemp?"

"Yeah. That's what he said."

"Okay. You drove him to the John Radcliffe?" Goodall asked.

"Yeah, so it would seem I did. I didn't know the name of the hospital until I saw the name on the signs at the edge of the town."

"Where did you go?"

"Go where?" Tom asked.

"When you drove away from the hospital?"

"First, I saw he was being looked after…"

"Why did you leave in a hurry?" Goodall asked.

"Truth is. It's not my car."

"Whose car is it?"

"My friends."

"Does your friend have a name?"

"Leroy Panther."

"Did Mister Panther know you had his car?"

"Yeah, sure."

"You had his permission?" Goodall asked.

"Yes. But I don't have insurance. That's one of the reasons I decided to beat it."

"What's the other?"

"I didn't want to get involved," replied Tom candidly and truthfully.

"What changed your mind?" Goodall asked.

"I told Leroy about the events. He advised me to call you straight away."

"He's a wise man. Did you notice any other vehicles in the lay-by?"

"Yeah. There were two. One at the beginning of the stretch, one at the other end. I parked between them."

"We located one of the vehicles this morning. It's registered to a Mister Kemp. Was he carrying anything?"

"Carrying?"

"Yeah. A bag. A weapon. Anything?"

"No, he had his hands clamped to his stomach. Can I ask a question?" Tom asked.

"What is it?"

"I understand that the man died."

"That's correct. He died overnight of his wounds," the detective confirmed.

"Oh, my God. He's dead," Tom said under his breath. "Do you have the person who shot him?" he asked.

The detective didn't respond for a moment, then just said a quick, firm. "No. We don't."

"Will you be wanting to interview me?"

"Of course. We'll also need to recover the vehicle you were driving for forensic analysis. What's your address?"

Tom gave him his home address.

"We'll have someone with you as soon as we can get there. Where is the car?"

Tom turned to Leroy and gave him a blank face. "Outside my house. Right now."

"Leave it there. We'll have someone with you shortly. Thanks for calling. Just give me your full name again and your date of birth for the record."

Tom gave him his full name again and his date of birth.

Tom hung up the telephone, then ran his hands over his head. He stepped into the front room with Riana and Leroy following him.

"If I was you I'd play it with a straight bat," said Leroy, using one of his favourite cricket metaphors.

"I absolutely intend to," said Tom. He sat on the sofa, crossed his legs, and waited for the police to arrive at his home.

Chapter 5

The police descended on the Scott house one and a half hours after the telephone conversation. The man leading the team was the man he had spoken to on the telephone. Chief Detective Inspector Derek Goodall of the Thames Valley police service was a rather sober looking fifty-year-old. Typical detective material. He was wearing a green Burberry coat over a beige jacket, and grey trousers.

He was well-rounded in both physical outlook and intellect. He was at least six-one tall and adequately built but not excessively overweight. The belt around his trousers wasn't straining. He spoke with a kind of middle England accent that suggested he was very much local to the Oxford area. He played it with a straight bat, though it looked as if he had not played cricket for some time. His partner was a forty something female officer by the name of DI Mel Drake. Tom assumed her name was either Melody or Melanie. She didn't tell him. She let DCI Goodall do most of the talking in the first instance.

She was a rather masculine type who didn't look quite right in the trouser suit and the black ankle length boots on her feet. Her short-cropped hair gave her quite a brusque appearance. They were accompanied by another plain clothed detective who introduced himself as DI Barry Holmes. He was from the local west London constabulary.

Knowing that his car was going to be confiscated, Leroy Panther had decided to go home, before the police arrived, and leave them to it.

Tom showed them the Mercedes which was parked on the hard-standing outside his house. DI Holmes asked DI Drake to arrange for the Thames Valley force to come out with a low-loader to collect the car and have it transported to Oxford where the local forensic team would examine it from top to bottom.

Tom opened the car doors and showed them the inside. He repeated that it wasn't his car. He told them that he had cleaned the inside this morning, though the blood stain on the passenger seat was still fresh. He knew the police would be able to do a DNA test to match the blood of the dead man to confirm that he had been in the car.

After showing them the car, Tom took the three officers into his home. He introduced them to Riana. He noticed how they each took the time to take in the ambience and the quirky decoration and the colour scheme with its over emphasis on the green, yellow, and red shades and the art work on the walls and the cubist pieces of sculpture Riana had made at a local art crafts workshop. DI Drake said she was impressed, though Tom detected that she was saying that to create a cozier, friendly atmosphere. One that was more conducive to getting answers to the questions they wanted to ask him.

Tom and Riana were sitting together on the sofa. DCI Goodall was in the armchair. DI Holmes remained standing in the open doorframe leading into the kitchen and DI Drake parked her ample backside on a straight-backed chair next to the fireplace.

Both DCI Goodall and DI Drake made themselves comfortable then took notepads and pens out of their pockets. Goodall smiled. He made eye contact with Tom.

"Perhaps you'd like to start by giving us a full account of how you came to be near the lay-by on the A44 last night. You're not under suspicion or any caution so please speak freely. We need to establish a clear picture of what you heard and what you saw," he said.

His manner and approach were friendly and open. Just like the manner he had portrayed over the telephone.

"Sure. As I said. I'd been to a job interview in Worcester. I'm about to be made redundant from the place I work at. So, I've been looking for another job. I drove over there yesterday at around dinner time. One…"

"Perhaps you'd like to tell us about later," said DCI Goodall encouraging him to skip the peripherals and get straight to the incident.

"Okay. I had my interview at about four-thirty. There was a delay because one of the other applicants was delayed by an accident on the motorway. The interview took about an hour. I left the place at five-thirty, then I managed to land right in the middle of that rain. The weather last night was awful, so I didn't rush back," he said.

"Great for a transport distribution manager. Won't you say," said Riana in a wry tone of voice that contained an element of sarcasm.

DCI Goodall and DI Holmes forced a smile. DI Drake retained a business-like grin.

Tom continued. "Anyway, I managed to head towards Oxford. I was driving a car I wasn't familiar with, so I took it easy. After thirty minutes or so when I knew I wasn't far from the M40 I decided to take a break and have a cig, so I pulled into the long lay-by just before a place called Yanton."

DI Holmes cleared his throat with a light cough. "How many other cars where in the lay-by?" he asked.

Tom glanced at him for the briefest of moments, then looked away and focused his eyes back on DCI Goodall. "It was pitch black. I could hardly see a thing and the light was hardly strong enough to light the tarmac. I recall passing one car, went passed it for about twenty yards, then pulled in. There was another car further ahead close to the turn back onto the road."

"Did you notice the registration numbers?" Goodall asked.

"No. As I said it was too dark," replied Tom.

"What then?" DI Holmes asked.

"I found my cigs and a lighter. I was going to light up in the car, but it's not my car. Its Riana's brothers. I knew he'd go ballistic if he smelt tobacco smoke in the car, so I got out and stretched my legs. I needed a breath of fresh air anyway. I got out of the car and lit up."

"Was there much traffic on the road?"

"No. It was quiet. It had stopped raining cats and dogs."

"Okay," said DCI Goodall. "How long before you heard the gunshots?" he asked.

"About twenty to thirty seconds, maybe a minute I'd guess."

"How close to you were they?" DI Drake asked.

"Difficult to tell. I looked into the trees but couldn't see a thing. It was thick with shrubs and what-have-you."

"How far apart were the sounds?" DI Holmes asked.

"The shots?" Tom asked.

"Yes."

"About ten…maybe fifteen seconds."

"Did you hear any shouts? Any voices or any other sounds?"

All the time they were talking, Tom was thinking about the black sports bag in the bottom of the blanket box which was in the room directly above his head. The one that contained half a million pounds in cash.

"No. Nothing like that," he replied.

"Then what?" DCI Goodall asked.

"I assumed they were coming from a farmer's field or some place, so I didn't think much about it. I was smoking a cig, so I concentrated on that."

"You didn't see any fire from a muzzle then?" DCI Goodall asked.

"No. Nothing. I couldn't see anything, but I heard the sounds."

DI Drake was continuing to make notes, but DCI Goodall wasn't. He seemed to be content to let someone else take the record.

"How long before Kemp appeared out of the wooded area?" Goodall asked.

"About another twenty seconds. Thirty tops," Tom replied.

"What was your initial thought?" DI Holmes asked.

Tom shrugged his shoulders. "I wondered who on earth it was and what he was doing there. Maybe he'd gone in there for a piss or summat. He came through a gap in the fence, over the grass verge and came along the path. He was staggering as if he'd had a few too many. But as he got nearer I saw the blood."

"Did he say anything?" Goodall asked.

"No. Not at first. He was sort of panting and groaning at the same time...."

"But he told you his name. Didn't he?" DI Drake asked, as if she was seeking to catch him out.

"In the car. When he was settled. I asked him his name and he said it was Lyle Kemp." Tom said in a believable strong tone of voice.

DI Drake wrote something into her notebook.

Tom looked at Goodall. "Can I ask a question?"

Goodall didn't reply immediately. He looked slightly hesitant. "What is it?" he asked after the pause.

"What's all this about?" Tom asked.

"What's all what about?" Goodall asked.

"The shooting. Is this guy known to you?"

"The victim?"

"Yes," said Tom.

"Why do you ask?" DI Holmes asked.

"I'm curious. It's not every day of the week that you stop to have a smoke then you find yourself hearing gun shots then having to tend to someone who's been shot."

Goodall's body language stiffened. "We're keeping an open mind at the moment," he said.

That was police code for they didn't have a clue, or they had loads of clues, but weren't prepared to share them.

Goodall glanced at Riana then back to Tom. "One last question for the time being. Are you adamant that he wasn't carrying anything in his hand?"

"Like what?"

"A bag of some description. A piece of luggage?"

Tom felt his throat going dry. "No. Maybe he dropped it as he was staggering through the bushes," he said.

"Maybe. But Mister Kemp kept muttering to the nurses as he was being wheeled into the theatre something about a bag and asking them where it was."

"Oh right. No, he never mentioned anything to me in the car," Tom said, keeping his nerve and his voice clear and unwavering.

"Okay," said Goodall. He looked at his watch, then put his eyes back on Tom. "We need you to do something for us."

"What's that?" Tom asked.

"We need you to accompany us to the scene to establish exactly where you were standing when you heard the shots and where the other cars were parked. Can you accompany us to the scene?"

"What now?" Tom asked.

"Yes."

"Do I have much choice?" he asked.

Both DCI Goodall and DI Holmes glanced at each other.

"You have the right to refuse, but you'd really be helping us with our enquiries," said DI Holmes.

Tom knew in a heartbeat that he had made a mistake. By his sudden reluctance to cooperate he had in effort shone a light on himself. He had to quickly backtrack and gloss over the error of judgement. He didn't want them to know he had something to hide.

"Sorry. I misunderstood. I'd be pleased to accompany you. Not a problem at all," he said seeking to reduce suspicion on himself.

Goodall forced a smile. "Thanks. They'll be a truck along shortly to take the car in for examination. Where does the owner live? Mister Leroy Panther."

"He's in Acton."

"Does he have an address in Acton?"

Riana gave him her half-brother's address.

"Once we're done with the vehicle it will be returned to that address. Should be a couple of days. Maybe three at a guess," said DI Drake.

"Okay. Thanks, I'll tell my brother," said Riana.

Two minutes later Tom left with the police officers in their unmarked Audi saloon for the drive to the lay-by on the A44. Nothing was said in the car. Tom was on the back seat next to DI Drake. DI Holmes was driving with Goodall in the passenger seat next to him.

Tom was thinking about what he was going to do with the money. The police clearly had a suspicion that the victim had a bag of some description, though maybe they had no idea what it contained. Or maybe they knew Lyle Kemp and had a clear picture of what had happened and what had gone on in the lay-by. Maybe they already had the shooter in custody.

He hoped that Riana, who had been in the room all the time would take the bag out of the blanket box and hide it somewhere. Like the loft, under the sheets of insulation might be a good place.

It took them around one hour and fifteen minutes to reach the outskirts of Oxford, drive through the city in the mid-day rush hour and get onto the A44 for the final two mile stretch to the lay-by.

Chapter 6

On arrival at the lay-by, Tom was in for a major surprise. Not only were there about half a dozen marked police cars parked there, but a mobile Thames Valley police investigation vehicle was in situ.

The lay-by was cordoned off by a line of tape with the words: 'Police Caution... Do Not Enter' stenciled across it. As the unmarked car approached the end of the lay-by, DI Holmes reduced speed. DCI Goodall opened the passenger side window and flashed his ID badge at the young copper manning the entrance. He unwrapped the tape from around a road sign pole and allowed DI Holmes to drive onto the lay-by.

He went by the mobile unit, pulled into the kerb then killed the engine. All four occupants got out of the car. Tom surveyed the scene. He was finding it hard to grasp the number of people and the resources that had been assigned to the case.

The late morning was fine, sunny and the air was crisp with the aroma from the nearby farmland. The overhanging canopy of trees and brushes were beginning to bud even at this early time of the year. The unusually warm, but damp weather of the past couple of days suggested that the spring was going to arrive early. Amen to that thought Tom. He wasn't a winter person.

He could hear people in the wooded area, probably cops who had been drafted in to comb through the undergrowth for evidence such as ejected cartridge cases and the like. The traffic on the A44, with the large police presence in the lay-by, was going passed at a respectable speed instead of the usual ten miles an hour over the speed limit. Most of the occupants of the vehicles were rubbernecking the activity in the lay-by.

With the mobile unit in place the pace of the investigation had ratcheted up a few notches. The victim, Lyle Kemp, had passed away from a gunshot so this was a murder scene, and while DCI Goodall said he was keeping an open mind, maybe, just maybe there was a lot more to this, than met the eye. Maybe there was a terrorism link. Maybe Lyle was a terrorist, or he had been shot by a terrorist. It was likely that it had nothing to do with terrorism, but it was a gangland settling of scores, though the lovely plains and fields of Oxfordshire were hardly renowned as a hotbed of gangland turf wars.

Goodall opened the door to the mobile unit, stepped inside and went out of view. That left DI's Drake and Holmes, with Tom on the roadway. Then Tom clapped his eyes on a civilian car parked further ahead. It was one of the two cars he had seen last night as he drove onto the lay-by. The car was a top-of-the-range Jaguar model, though it wasn't brand-new. Both the front doors were open, and the bonnet was up. At this moment in time there was no one around it, but clearly some officers had been inside examining the vehicle from top to bottom. He could only speculate that it was the car the victim had been driving. The first car he had passed wasn't there. Perhaps it had been the car the person who had shot Lyle Kemp had been driving. Could it have been an attempt at a car jack, gone wrong. If that was the case, then two people would have been involved. One to drive the car they had arrived in, the other to drive the stolen vehicle.

A couple of minutes passed. The sound of cops in the wooden area, searching through the terrain had decreased so it was quieter than it had been when he first arrived.

A further minute went by before DCI Goodall emerged from out of the unit with a prim looking female police officer in a white blouse, and dark trousers. She had a bow in the collar of the blouse. By the epaulettes on the blouse she looked to be the senior officer in these parts. She eyed Tom, through the lenses of a pair of black rimmed spectacles over her eyes, with a non-descript expression. She and Goodall moved closer to DI Holmes, DI Drake and Tom Scott.

"This is Tom Scott. The man who found the victim," said DCI Goodall, gesturing to Tom with a thrust of his head.

She stepped closer. "Deputy Chief Constable of Thames Valley police, Lena Hartley," she announced, introducing herself in a formal way. "I understand that you parked in this lay-by at around twenty to seven last night," she said.

Tom smiled at her, but she maintained a cold, hard expression on her face. "Yes. That's correct," he said.

"Can you show us exactly where you were when you observed Mister Kemp coming out of the trees?" Goodall asked.

"Certainly," said Tom. He stepped onto the path and moved the couple of yards or so to the concrete litter bin embedded in the grassy verge at the other side of the path. He stopped.

"About here," he said and turned to face into the wood. He could now see a line of people who were all dressed in dark overalls who were picking at the undergrowth with long sticks in their hands.

"What about the sound of gunshots? Can you recall which direction they came from?" Hartley asked.

Tom pointed at a fifteen-degree angle into the wood. "I think the first shot came from a spot approximately to my left," he said.

"What about the second?" she asked.

He moved his hand to the right. "About there," he said.

"How long was the gap between the sounds?" DCI Goodall asked.

"As I said before. It was ten to fifteen seconds at a guess."

"Did the shots sound the same?"

"One sounded slightly sharper than the other."

"So, two different firearms?" asked DCI Goodall.

Tom wasn't sure if that was a question aimed at him. He paused, until it was obvious, by the look on Goodall's face that the question was for him. "Yes, I'd say so. They made different sounds," he replied.

"Tell us about the second car."

"As I turned into the lay-by I passed a car."

"Can you remember the colour?"

"White."

"White?"

"Yeah."

"The model?" Hartley asked.

"To be honest all cars look the same to me. It was a four door, a saloon. Possibly a Ford. I don't know."

"What about the registration?" Goodall asked.

"It was pitch black."

"Can you take me to the spot where the car was parked?"

"Certainly." Tom led them twenty yards or so back along the path to the place where he thought the first car was parked. "About here," he said.

"And where was your car?" Goodall asked.

He looked back up the path and pointed ahead. "About the same place where that unit is," he replied.

"Could you see if there was any one in either of the cars?" Hartley asked.

"No. As I said it was pitch black and the windows were splattered with rain. I wouldn't have been able to see inside, unless I had walked right up to them and looked in."

"Did you wonder what the cars were doing parked here?" Goodall asked.

"No. Not really. Why should I? It was cold. Maybe the driver had stopped to take a leak or for a smoke or a nap. The rain last night was lashing down. The amount of spray coming up was making it difficult to concentrate so I stopped to wait for it to ease. As well as for a cig."

Neither Goodall or the top lady officer said anything. Tom had explained why he had stopped and it sounded like he was telling the truth. If they suspected that he had shot Lyle Kemp or that he was somehow involved, then there was no way of knowing. But he wasn't involved. He knew it and he suspected the police knew it as well.

The police officers remained mute for the next few seconds. DCI Goodall was about to say something, when there was a shout from just inside the lip of the trees. Someone had found something of importance. There was increased activity inside the perimeter. A uniformed officer who was wearing a paper overall came out of the mobile unit carrying what looked like a polythene bag. He stepped off the path, over the grass verge, through the gap in the railing and slipped into the cover of the trees.

DCI Goodall, DCC Hartley, and Tom walked back up the path towards the mobile unit. As they reached the centre of the path, another cop approached Hartley and Goodall.

"We've found a firearm in the undergrowth," he said. "It looks like a Walther PPK or a hybrid."

"Call off the search for now," DCC Hartley ordered. "Congratulate the officer who found the item," she said. "I think we've got a good idea what happened here," she added.

Tom watched as the man in the noddy suit came out of the wood carrying the polythene evidence bag with what looked like the black shape of a handgun nestling inside. The man made straight for the unit, stepped up a ladder, opened the door and went inside. DCC Hartley followed him inside.

The cop who had announced the discovery of the gun, then went into the cover of the trees and spoke to one of the senior officers who had a megaphone in his hand. He put it to his mouth and shouted, 'stand down,' at the top of his voice. The searching was over for the moment.

Little doubt, that the firearm would be quickly whisked to a ballistics unit somewhere in Oxford to be tested to determine if it had recently been fired. And to do an analysis to check if the slug taken out of the victim's body came from that firearm. If the answer to that was no, then the shooter still had the weapon that he used to kill Lyle Kemp. And more to the point, the killer was still at large.

A minute passed before DCI Goodall came to Tom. He thanked him for his assistance. He said he would be in touch if he needed to speak to him again.

DI Holmes drove Tom home. He was back in his home on Goldhawk Road, Shepherd's Bush within one hour of leaving the scene of the murder.

When he arrived home, he saw that Leroy's Mercedes C200 had gone from outside of the house. Riana informed him that the car had been winched onto a Thames Valley police low-loader and driven away. The driver of the wagon told her he had no idea when the car would be delivered to her half-brother's home – not that she was bothered. She was more concerned about emptying the sports bag and putting the wads of cash into a place the police or anyone else would ever think of looking.

She told Tom she had the perfect hiding place. Over the course of the next ten minutes, Tom and Riana emptied the holdall. Riana took a duvet from out of the airing cupboard on the landing. She painstakingly untacked the seam at one end, then the pair of them stuffed the forty-eight bundles of cash inside the thick spongy wading. Then Riana sewed the seam back together. She fed the duvet into a pastel coloured cover and clipped it into place, then she put the duvet back onto the top shelf of the airing cupboard.

That evening, after they had done some shopping at a local superstore, Tom took a walk into the car park. He shoved the empty sports bag into one of those metal charity cloths bank containers lining the edge of the car park.

Chapter 7

Monday 15th February

Several days elapsed without Tom receiving an update from the police. The incident had occurred last Tuesday night. The trip to the scene with the police had taken place the day after. By the following Monday, Tom was beginning to think that whilst he wasn't 'home and hosed' he wouldn't hear anything else from the likes of DCI Goodall until they had something to go on or something they wanted to share with him. He suspected that they did think he may have been far more involved in the episode than he was letting on.

Of course, he kept abreast of any latest development by checking the news on the internet every five hours, or so. The man who had died had been officially named as forty-six-year-old father of two, Lyle Kemp who resided in Highgate, north London. Geez, thought Tom, Kemp was only four years older than him. Losing his life at forty-six must have been an awful shock to his family and friends. Though as Tom was to discover from one report, Lyle Kemp was well-known to the police and did have a record for fencing stolen valuables. And we weren't talking about knocked off TVs or mobile phones. We were talking big league here, stolen gems, jewellery, and precious metals worth a great deal of money.

Whilst Tom didn't know anything about the trade in stolen jewellery he could only speculate that the incident in the wood was related to criminal activity. Maybe, the exchange of gunfire was as the result of a deal gone bad. Maybe the money in the bag was

Kemp's and he was using it to buy stolen merchandise. A heist on a Hatton Garden jewellery wholesaler had only occurred six weeks ago, over the Christmas period. Perhaps it had something to do with that. Of course, it was all down to maybe and perhaps with no guarantee that it was anywhere near the truth.

On the job front, Tom had received a letter in the post from the haulage firm in Worcester. He didn't get the job. He had been near to the top of the list, but they had offered it to someone else. They expressed their gratitude and commended him for his patience and everything else. If anything else came-up in the pipeline shortly they would consider him and give him a call. But they were 'extremely' sorry to inform him that he didn't get the job. To be honest he really didn't care. He had more pressing things on his mind, like the half a million pounds stuffed into the duvet in the cupboard on the landing.

Tuesday 16th February

Leroy Panther called Tom on Tuesday evening to tell him that the police had delivered his car to his home in Acton at two o'clock that afternoon. It just so happened that Marie was at home to receive it.

The police had given it a valet and given the bodywork a sparkling polish. They had even attached one of those lavender fragrance sachets to the rear-view mirror.

Despite the letter from the haulage firm, things were going okay for Tom. He had negotiated a good leaving package with the firm who were 'letting him go'. They told him he didn't have to return to work. He was free to leave now. He was pleased about that.

The lack of news and any update gave Tom and Riana an air of confidence and a feeling that they might get away with it. As the days passed then their level of optimism that they might be able to begin a new life in Trinidad increased. Nothing had happened which gave them any indication that they were about to be caught.

Sadly, that's not the way it proved to be. Tom and Riana received some devastating news on the morning of Wednesday 17th February. It shocked them to the core of their souls and told them this wasn't over by a long way.

Wednesday 17th February

It was ten o'clock in the morning when Tom took a telephone call from someone who said he was a police officer based in Paddington Green police station in west London.

"Okay," said Tom. He immediately assumed it was a follow-up call.

"Can I speak to Riana Thomas?" the officer asked.

"No. Not at the moment," said Tom. He was suspicious that the man who said he was a police officer, wasn't anything of the sort.

"In that case. Can you pass on some important news to her regarding her brother a Mister Leroy Panther?" the supposed police officer asked.

"Yes. I can."

"I'm sorry to inform you, but he's gravely ill in Ealing Hospital."

Tom was stunned. He couldn't say a word for a long moment. He couldn't think straight. "Ill?" he muttered in reply. "Leroy?"

"Yes. *Gravely* ill," said the caller stressing 'gravely' with an inflection of tone.

"How?"

"Sorry, but what's your name?"

Again, Tom was suspicious that the man wasn't who he said he was. He had heard a recent story of how someone impersonating a police officer had tried to get someone's bank details. Was this guy trying to hoodwink him into believing he was a police officer?

"Did you say Ealing Hospital?" Tom asked.

"Yes."

"I'll call them myself." Tom said, then he terminated the call before the 'police officer' could utter another word.

Riana worked part-time, for five hours a day, four days a week, in a sandwich bar on Uxbridge Road, right opposite Shepherd's Bush Green. Tom called her on her mobile phone. He informed her about the content of the supposed message from the police but expressed his suspicion that it could have been a hoax. Riana advised him to call Leroy's mobile to see if he could speak to him. If he didn't have any joy she had a telephone number for Marie Slater, Leroy's partner. Riana said she would call the police in Paddington Green.

He said, 'good idea'. He immediately called Leroy's mobile, but it rang and rang without him picking up. That was unusual, Leroy usually picked-up on the fifth or sixth ring. If he didn't answer, it went to voice mail, but on this occasion, it just rang and rang. Tom terminated the call. As he put the telephone down Riana, called back.

"I've just called the police in Paddington Green," she said. Her tone of voice was grave. "It's true, I've spoken to a Sergeant Naomi Porter. Both Leroy and Marie are in Ealing Hospital."

"Geez," said Tom. "What do you know?" he enquired.

"Two men broke into their home in the early hours of the morning and attacked them both. Marie was bound and gagged and tied to a chair. Leroy was attacked and beaten so badly he's…" she was almost crying as she spoke… "in Intensive Care with severe injuries."

"Oh my God," said Tom. "I can't believe it. How was the alarm raised?"

"Marie managed to free the gag from around her mouth. She shouted for help. Luckily her next door neighbour heard her shouting."

"What time was this?" Tom asked.

"About four-fifty this morning," Riana replied.

"Geez." Tom repeated. "How's Leroy?" he asked.

Riana didn't respond for a few long moments. It was as if she was summoning the mental strength to tell him. She managed to pull up the courage. "Leroy's injuries are bad. They've had to put him into an induced coma."

"Oh my God," said Tom.

"I'm coming home," said Riana. "We had better get to the hospital to see them and try to find out what happened."

"I'll phone for a cab and pick you up. Then we'll get to the hospital," said Tom.

"Okay," she said, then terminated the call.

He called a local taxi company for a cab to take him from his home, first to the 'Salt and Pepper' sandwich bar on Uxbridge Road, then to Ealing Hospital.

Chapter 8

Ealing Hospital was a large district hospital in Southall, serving all parts of north-west London. Tom had been in there for a minor operation on his ankle when he broke it playing football more than ten years ago. The main buildings were in a three-block structure, the tallest was a ten-floor high office like structure. It was a typical nineteen-sixties block style construction set in a parcel of land several acres wide.

The cab took them straight to the main entrance of the Accident and Emergency unit. Typical of a busy hospital, a wide assortment of people were coming and going from the entrance with the usual sounds and smells associated with an environment of this kind.

Tom was apprehensive. He wondered what had occurred. Was it linked to the death of Lyle Kemp? Or was it a total coincidence? Perhaps the burglars had chosen the house at random. He did fear seeing how Leroy looked and whether he would be able to tell him if his attackers had said anything to him. Also, if the police would be there and want to speak to him.

Once inside the glass-foyer entrance Riana marched straight up to the reception desk where staff were sitting behind a windowed counter. She spoke to a receptionist who immediately consulted a computer monitor and tapped in a few commands. She typed the name, Leroy Panther into the search facility.

It transpired that Leroy had been brought in at five-twenty-six this morning. He was in the Intensive Care unit. His condition was described as 'stable'. Riana asked about Marie. The receptionist told her that she had been released at nine-thirty, therefore she might be in the transport area waiting to be taken home.

Riana asked her if they could go to the unit to see Leroy. First, the receptionist wanted to know who they were. After some 'humming and arrin' she called an internal number and spoke to the unit manager. It was against hospital protocol, but a doctor agreed to speak to them. If they went to the unit entrance, they would be met by a doctor who would update them on Leroy's condition. The receptionist directed them down a long glass-encased, light filled corridor, through the door at the bottom, turn left and the ICU entrance was at the end of the corridor by a pair of security-controlled doors. Someone would be at the door to greet them.

Riana thanked the receptionist. She and Tom set off to find the unit. The hospital in this part of the building was surprisingly quiet. Few people, except for those in hospital garb were going back and forth through the corridors.

When they reached the entrance to the Intensive Care Unit they could see a young woman in a long white coat, standing by a pair of closed doors that led into the unit. She had a stethoscope around her neck and a clipboard in her hand.

Above the door was a sign saying: 'Intensive Care Unit – No entry'. The plastic name badge attached to the pocket of her coat told them that she was Doctor Anna Guppta. She was a nice-looking young lady with shinny bright eyes and a nice smile. She wore her hair up and tied back by a bow. She had a doctor's poise and presence about her.

"Are you the relatives of Leroy Panther?" she asked Riana, perhaps noticing the family resemblance or maybe she just guessed.

"Yes. How is my brother?" she asked hurriedly.

The doctor's expression changed from one of non-description to one of serious concern. "He's extremely ill," she said with an air of understatement and in an appropriate soft tone of voice. "He's had a blow to his head that has caused trauma and swelling to the brain, which is why we've put him in an induced coma."

"He'll be okay? Won't he?" Tom asked.

"I would advise caution at this time." The doctor replied, carefully picking her words, as if to stress the seriousness of his injuries. Nevertheless, her words came like a hammer blow.

"What do you mean?" Tom asked bluntly.

"He may not survive," she replied in an equally blunt manner.

Riana began to sob. Tom put his arm around her and held her tight.

"We're doing everything we can. We hope for a good outcome, but please prepare yourself for the worst," said the doctor in a candid manner.

Tom drew in a deep breath. He tightened his arms around Riana then stroked her hair. Losing Leroy would be a catastrophe, that no amount of money no matter how great could soften. It would be a blow they wouldn't get over for a very long time. If it had something to do with the money, Tom would forever regret borrowing Leroy's car. It was as if he was in a bad dream. It didn't seem real. It was a surreal feeling. Like he was experiencing an outer body experience. He could see by the look on Dr Guppta's face and by her tone of voice that Leroy's chances of survival were probably evenly stacked at fifty-fifty.

"Have the police been here?" Tom asked.

"They came in with the victim," she said. "Once he was placed into this unit they questioned Mrs. Panther before they left."

He was going to tell her that there wasn't a Mrs. Panther but thought better of it.

"Can we see him?" Riana asked.

The doctor considered her request for a moment. "I don't see why not. Follow me. This way."

She placed her ID badge in a card reader by the door and the doors instantly moved inward. She led them inside, around a central management area, then through a ward with beds on either side behind lines of green curtained cubicles. There little sound except for the whirring of a machine and the blast of an AC unit. Nurses, both male and female in dark blue tops and matching trousers were going about their business. At one end of the unit were several small rooms which housed the most serious cases. Tom was aware of the smell of carbolic soap and the gleaming sparkling cleanliness of the room. There wasn't a stain or a discarded piece of paper anywhere. Despite this he still didn't like the environment. It was where car crash victims came to die and those clinging to life were given the last rites.

Dr Guppta turned into the area in front of the line of single rooms. Each room had a long window looking out onto the ward, but the inside view was closed off by vertically drawn blinds. She went to the door of a room, opened it, and stepped inside. There was a bed against the back wall with a plethora of monitoring machines around it. Leroy Panther was laid on the bed. His naked chest, down to a point just below his navel was exposed. His arms were rigid down by his sides. He was still and utterly motionless. There was a transparent tube in his mouth connected to one of the monitor machines placed at one side of the bed. The sight of a gravely-ill Leroy hit Tom with a sense of utter hopelessness.

Riana approached her half-brother. She couldn't do anything but let the tears roll out of her eyes. It was a natural response when seeing a loved one in mortal danger and close to death. Her screams were trapped inside her chest. It was as if she didn't want to let them out in case she offended the doctor or woke up her half-brother.

"Oh Leroy. What in God's name happened to you?" she asked in a semi whisper.

There were several red welts on his chest where he had been hit with an object of some description, or maybe a fist. There was bruising around both his eyes and the mark of an indentation on his forehead, but little else. He wasn't covered in bandages or wading of any kind.

There were sticky patches attached to his upper chest with wires attached to the machines monitoring his vital organs. A monitoring device was attached to the tip of his right-hand index finger. The machines were making a low humming sound, but there was no obvious indication that they were keeping him alive. He appeared to be breathing on his own. Which was a good sign.

"Will he survive?" Riana asked.

Dr Guppta looked at the patient. She didn't meet Riana eyes. "I don't know for sure. It will be touch and go, but at least he's a fit man. Anyone less physically fit may have succumbed," she said. Riana put her hand to her mouth to stop a cry escaping. Dr Guppta stepped a pace towards her patient. "He's in an induced coma, but he could show signs of recovery at any time. The blow to his forehead does give me concern, but he might come out of it, or never at all. We'll have a better idea later today and in the coming days," she said.

"What's an induced coma?" Tom asked.

"It's something we do to decrease the pressure on the brain when it has been subject to swelling. This way the brain is effectively put into a sleep mode," she said.

Just then the door to the room came open and a female nurse stepped into the room. She smiled at Riana and Tom, then she went about her business. She took the clip board attached to the end of the bed, went to the monitoring machines, took the readings, and made some notes on the papers attached to the clip board.

Tom looked at Leroy. "He's in the best place," he said in an effort to comfort Riana.

She didn't reply but stepped close to the bed and looked down into her brother's face.

"Come on sweetheart," she whispered to him. "You'll come out of this." She took his hand, opened his fingers, and threaded her hand in his, then she leaned over and kissed him on the cheek.

There wasn't a great deal more they could do, but to wait and see what developed. A gentle giant was sleeping. He would surely soon wake up, rip off the wires from his chest, get out of bed and walk out of here.

"Can we wait here?" Riana asked Dr Guppta.

"No, I'm sorry. That's not permitted in this unit. You can wait in the reception area if you want to. We'll contact you immediately should there be any development in his condition."

Tom was going to ask her what condition meant but didn't.

"Leave your contact details at the front desk," the nurse advised.

"We'll do that," said Tom. He reached forward, took Riana by the arm, and gently pulled her away from the bed. Doctor Guppta led them out of the room, back through the ward and out of the exit.

Dr Guppta said the nurse was correct in every way. The best thing to do was to go home and let them do their job and wait for any news. Hopefully, it would be good, but she had to play both sides of the coin. By the lack of bruises and signs of trauma inflicted on his body, Tom was relieved that he wasn't black and blue, but clearly something devastating had happened to him.

Riana did as the nurse advised. She left her details at the front counter in the reception area. They left the unit five minutes later and once outside headed to a taxi-rank in the car park. Their next stop was to Leroy's house in Acton to see his partner Marie.

Chapter 9

Marie Slater and Leroy Panther resided on a quiet street in a quiet part of Acton in a quiet part of prime west London suburbia. Tom asked the taxi driver to drop them off outside of number fifty-eight. The house was a semi-detached three-bedroom dwelling with a red tiled roof and bowed windows, top and bottom. It was standard for the area and the street, which was full of hardworking, tax paying, working-class people trying to make ends meet in tricky economic times.

There was a drive on the side of the house. A works van which displayed a glass repairer business logo was parked close to the gated wall. Leroy's Mercedes C200 was nowhere to be seen. As the house didn't have a garage then it was safe to assume that the car wasn't here. There was also no evidence of a police presence.

The taxi dropped Riana and Tom outside. He paid the fare. During the twenty-minute journey from the hospital both he and Riana had said few words to each other. The driver had tried to make some conversation, but when Tom didn't reply to a question he soon got the message.

Riana pressed the doorbell in the door frame and waited for Marie to appear. Marie opened the door within a few seconds of the chime ringing. She greeted them with the look of someone who hadn't had any sleep for a while. She looked really worn out and downbeat. No surprise when you consider what she had been through. She had been held captive by two men. The house had been invaded and her partner was in hospital on the critical list. It couldn't get much worse than that. By the look of the patches of red around her eyes she had been crying. Her usual well-kept long red hair was disheveled, and it looked as if she had dressed in haste.

Marie Slater was an Australian citizen. She had a sparkling bubbly personality. A dry Aussie wit and a caustic sense of humour. She called a spade a spade. When it wasn't a spade it was a shovel, as Leroy had remarked on numerous occasions.

She had come to London from Sydney twelve years ago to set up home with a Brit she had met in a Sydney-side pub. She was what could have been called, 'a hostess' in a King's Cross club. It was her job to entice the punters inside to part with their cash.

When the relationship with the guy went south after a couple of years she decided to return home, but then she met Leroy. He persuaded her to stay in London. They had lived as husband and wife for the past ten years in this very house.

She showed them into the lounge. A lady was sitting on the sofa with a mug of something in her hand. Two men in work-gear, from a local glass repair company were fitting a sheet of ply-wood over a gap in one of the sliding patio doors that led onto decking at the rear of the house. The burglars had clearly come over the fence at the bottom of the garden, walked across the back garden and entered the house through the doors. It was the most obvious and easiest method of entry. Anyone with the tools and the gumption could easily force the lock that secured the door into the frame. Though

Tom was no expert he assumed the burglars were professionals as they had clearly come prepared to get into the house.

Some of the drawers in a writing bureau were still wide open and there were papers and items of paperwork scattered over the floor.

Marie sat down on the sofa, at the other side of the unknown lady who smiled at Riana and Tom. "I'm Louisa from next door. I heard Marie shouting for help this morning. Luckily, we heard her and came around."

"Thanks," said Riana. "I'm Riana. Marie's sister-in-law."

Louisa shrugged her shoulders. "It was nothing. We're very concerned, but at least the police have been here and the men…" she looked towards the two guys working on the door… "are doing an emergency repair. I must be going Marie. I'll see you later love."

Marie thanked Louisa and with that she got up off the sofa.

Tom thanked her. She tried to smile, but just nodded her head solemnly, then left the house.

Riana sat next to Marie, whilst Tom remained standing in the doorway. He watched the two men fit a sheet of plywood into the frame where the glass had been. The entire shattered panel was lying on the patio in several broken pieces.

"Have the police been gone long?" asked Riana.

"In the…in the," she repeated as if she was in shock and was finding it difficult to string two words together… "In the past thirty minutes," she said.

On a table at one side of the room were several documents and papers the burglars must have pulled from out of the drawers of the chest and the bureau, though they could have been insurance documents Marie had taken out to examine.

"We've been to the hospital and seen Leroy. We're praying for him," said Riana.

"He's as strong as an ox," said Marie. "If anyone can pull through it will be Leroy Panther."

Riana reached out and put her arm around Marie's shoulders and gave her a hug.

"Can you tell us what happened?" Tom asked.

Riana glanced at him with a withering face and gave him one of those 'not now' looks. Maybe she was right, maybe it was too early to be asking questions. The very kind of questions the police would have been asking her.

Marie blew out a deep sigh. "Two men broke in at around three-thirty this morning."

"Did you see their faces?" Tom asked.

"They were wearing balaclavas with holes for the eyes. They had baseball caps pulled low over their heads."

"Did they say anything?" he asked.

"Plenty."

"What like?"

"They kept asking for the money. Over and over again."

"What money?"

"I don't know. One of them had a knife. He put it to Lee's throat. Said if he didn't tell him where the money was, he was going to stab him in the throat."

Tom winced. "Did they have any kind of accent?" he asked.

"They weren't foreigners. They were definitely locals."

"All they kept asking about was some money?" Riana asked.

Marie raised her head for the first-time and looked directly at her. "Something about they knew he had the money and he had better tell them where it was."

"The money?" Tom asked.

"Yeah. The money," she repeated.

"What did Leroy say?" Riana asked. As if she wanted to get off the money trail.

"Said, he didn't know what they were on about. That's when one of them hit him on the head with a cosh. It half knocked him out."

"Geez," said Tom and visibly shuddered.

"They threatened us. They tied me to that chair over there." She thrust her head towards a straight backed wooden dining chair. "Then they began searching through the house looking for something." Her accent still contained a trace of her Aussie upbringing, though it had been softened by years of living in London.

"The money you were supposed to have," Tom said.

"Yeah, I guess that was it," Marie replied.

"How long where they here?"

"Too bloody long." She blew out a long sigh as if she was becoming tired with these questions. "About twenty to thirty minutes I'd say. Maybe more. They put a blindfold over my eyes and gagged me."

She put her hand to her face and began to sob. Riana pulled her close, gave her another hug and held her tight.

"It will be okay," she said. "You see. He'll be fine."

Tom took a deep breath of his own. He concluded that Leroy had not told Marie that he'd been using his car. If he had she might have questioned him about why he had been using it. Clearly the whole episode must have had something to do with the half a million-quid hidden in their airing cupboard.

The two guys fitting the plyboard into the empty panel hadn't batted an eyelid. They just carried on, doing what they were paid to do. Using a couple of delicate taps with a hammer they soon had the sheet inserted into the panel. The catch that secured the lock into the frame had been smashed. To secure the door they had wrapped half-a-reel of gaffer tape around the handle and the locking device. Once this was done the lead guy announced that they had finished for the time being, but that they would be back the following day with a fresh piece of glass to fit into the panel. And with that they collected their tools and left the house.

As soon as they had gone Marie seemed to have recovered some of her composure, but she was obviously subdued and suffering from a form of post-traumatic stress. She dapped her eyes with a tissue, then ran a hand through her mane of red hair.

"Marie. I noticed that the Mercedes isn't here," said Tom.

"They took it," she said.

"Who took it?" The police?" he asked.

"No. Those who broke in."

"Why would they take the car?" he asked.

"I've no idea."

"Don't worry about the car," said Riana. "We'll get you a new one."

Marie looked at her with a questioning face. Riana knew in that instant that she had made a mistake saying that.

"I'm just about to get a good redundancy package from my employer," Tom said. "We'll replace the car," he added.

Marie didn't say anything.

"What did those two bastards do to Leroy?" Tom asked, purposely changing the subject.

"They took him back upstairs to search through everything. I heard a fight. Leroy must have clobbered one of them. Next thing they must have hit him on the head again with the cosh. Then they came down and threatened me. All the time they were asking about the money. I said we didn't have any money in the house. Only credit cards. They asked me again and again. I said for Christ's sake we don't have any money in the house. It's all in the bank. What we have - ten thousand if we're lucky. After that they got the message and went. They must have taken the car keys off the key holder in the kitchen. I could hear them driving the car off the drive."

Tom looked at Riana and chewed on his bottom lip. He was now convinced, more than ever, that it related to the incident in the lay-by. These guys were professional criminals who were determined to find the money. He had no idea how they were connected to Lyle Kemp. Whether they were colleagues or adversaries of his.

"What did the police have to say?" he asked.

Riana looked aghast at him. "I think Marie has answered enough of our questions," she snapped at him. "She needs to rest," she added.

"No, I'm fine," Marie said. "I've got to face up to it. I want to talk. They're carrying out their investigation and said they will get back to me once they have something to report."

"Did they leave you with a contact name or number?" Tom asked.

Marie took a business card out of her cardigan pocket and put it to her eyes. "If I need to contact anyone. He's called Detective Chief Inspector Phillip May in Paddington Green police station."

"Okay. That's good," said Tom. "At least you've got a contact," he added.

There was a period of silence that lasted for ten seconds. Riana got up from the sofa and put her eyes on the open drawers in the bureau and the documents scattered on the dining table. "Let us make a start to get this tidied up," she said, looking at Tom. "We need it back too smart for when Leroy gets back home." There was a nuance of hope in her voice.

After twenty minutes clearing up, everything that had been scattered by the burglars was back in its rightful place. A couple of black marks on a wall were washed off with soapy water, but the trauma of been invaded by a couple of thugs would never fade. No amount of soap and water would wash away the memories. Now it was a case of hoping that the police would quickly apprehend the villains. Maybe they already had an idea who they were or maybe they didn't have a clue.

Riana suggested to Marie that she stay the night with them. Marie thanked her but turned down the offer saying she had already been invited to stay the night with her neighbour, Louisa. While it was very unlikely that the burglars would return, you could never be sure. Therefore, safety first was the priority.

Riana and Tom eventually left the house at eight o'clock in the evening, eight hours after arriving. They went home to their house in Shepherd's Bush.

Chapter 10

On arriving back home, Riana made a cup of tea and Tom made them both a sandwich then they went into the front room. Riana crashed onto the sofa. Tom sat in the armchair. They just looked at each other for a full minute, neither of them said a word. Riana looked shattered by the experience that had befallen her. Her half-brother was in hospital on the critical list and her sister-in-law was in bits and pieces.

"What are we going to do?" Tom asked.

She looked at him quizzically. "What do you mean?"

"About the money."

"Like what?"

"Give it to the police? Tell them everything."

"Are you kidding?" she asked. "We've got money for the first time in our grotty little life's and you want to give it back. You're having a laugh!"

"No!"

"Why?" she asked.

"Because we could be next in line for a visit."

"Maybe. But what we don't do is give in," she said.

Tom looked at the frames containing the photographs of Marley and Lennon. "They wouldn't approve," he said.

"Who?"

"Bob Marley and John Lennon."

"I don't suppose their other halves had to work in a crappy sandwich shop in Shepherd's Bush. And I don't reckon they ever lost their jobs as a haulage distribution manager." She scoffed. She could be caustic at times.

She had a point, he thought. He stayed non-committal. He didn't want to admit that she was right.

"What I want to know is who are those two men," Riana said.

"They must be connected to this Lyle Kemp fella. They have to be," he said.

"Why?" she asked.

"Who the hell would break into Leroy's place asking for the money. They thought that the money Kemp was carrying ended up with him."

"How?" she asked.

"Think about it. I used his car."

"But how did they know whose car it is?" she asked.

"They must have got the registration number."

"How?"

"Who knows. Maybe they saw me driving away. They made a note of the registration."

"How would they find out who was the owner of the car?" she asked.

"Easy. They pay someone working in an insurance brokers office. They bribe a copper to search the DVLA database. Easy. They get the address and think Leroy is me."

She knew he was on the right line. "So, they assume Leroy has the money that's in our airing cupboard?" she said.

"That's right," he replied.

"How do you think those two are connected to the man who died?" she asked.

"He was a dealer in stolen jewellery and that type of thing. Maybe he was selling, or he was buying. Think about it. The deal goes tits-up. Maybe he was trying to stiff them. Maybe he was buying. Not selling. One of them draws a gun and shoots Kemp. He fires back. I reckon they found his gun when I was at the lay-by with that Goodall and Drake. If the bullet they take out of him doesn't match the gun, then they will know that he was shot by someone else. They might be able to match it to a firearm."

"You seem to know a lot about guns," she commented.

"Not really. I knew watching all those cop shows would pay off one day."

"What are we doing to do?" she asked.

"I asked you that question a minute ago," he said.

"I know."

"Let me think about it."

Tom took his ham and pickle sandwich and took an enormous bite. Riana did likewise. They consumed their food in a silence that lasted five minutes.

After they had consumed their snack they resumed their conversation. Tom suggested that the best course of action would be to contact DI Phillip May at Paddington Green station to put him in the picture. A reluctance to speak to him might be construed as an attempt to keep a lid on things. He would tell him that the burglary and attack on his brother-in-law was probably linked to the murder of Lyle Kemp. There was a chance that the Met police had already been in contact with their colleagues in Oxford to discuss the case, but of course Tom had no way of knowing. He also had no way of knowing if Leroy had told the two men that it was his mate, Tom Scott, who had been driving his car last Tuesday, not him. If he had and if he had given them his address, then they might be planning to attack him. He didn't discuss this possibility with Riana. He wanted to keep it quiet. He was thinking about maybe getting out of London for a couple of days, but with Leroy in hospital and Marie needing their help that was a non-starter.

Anyway, the police might think they were running because they had something to hide. He instantly put that idea into the garbage bin. If they did get a visit later this evening or the following morning then they might have little option, but to give the men the money.

Tom said he would call the Met police in Paddington Green in the morning and speak to DI Phillip May.

Thursday 18th February

By a strange quirk of fate before Tom could make a telephone call to speak to DI May. He received an unannounced visit to his home from DI Barry Holmes.

Riana hadn't been out of the house long when Tom heard a knock at the front door. It was an early call. Eight-twenty in the morning. Riana had left home for the 'Salt and Pepper' sandwich shop at eight sharp to assist with the breakfast shift.

DI Holmes had brought a colleague along with him, non-other than DI Phillip May from Paddington Green. Holmes introduced him to Tom. DI May was a fair skinned, fair haired guy with beady eyes, high cheek bones and sunken jowls. An anemic looking man. DI Holmes was carrying a manila A4 size envelope under his right arm.

"This is some coincidence," said Tom has he showed them into the house and into the front room.

DI Holmes looked at him for an explanation. "Why is that?" he asked.

"I was about to call DI May to speak to him," he replied.

"What about?" DI May asked.

Tom looked into his eyes which were almost circular in shape. His fair hair was neatly cut across his forehead. He looked clean cut.

"I was talking to my sister-in-law, Marie Slater, last night and she said that you are the officer leading the investigation into the attack on her and my brother-in-law, Leroy Panther."

"That's right," he said in a clear and precise tone.

"It may have something to do with the murder of Lyle Kemp..."

"That's why we're here," Holmes injected. "We're already aware of the connection. Whoever broke in, and we've got our suspicions who it was – is at the top of our list of suspects in the murder. We think that whoever broke in thought that Leroy Panther was the driver of the car and that he took Lyle Kemp to the hospital in Oxford."

"That's what I was thinking," said Tom.

DI Holmes gave him something of a deadpan face that suggested his suspicion alert had been activated. "Miss Slater told us that the men who broke in were looking for money."

"I know. She told me," said Tom.

"So, when did you speak to her?" DI May asked.

"As soon as we received the news that Leroy was in hospital. We raced straight around to the hospital to see him." Neither of the detectives replied. "After we'd been there we went to visit Marie. After all Riana is her sister-in-law and they're pretty close."

"Where is she today?" DI May asked.

"Who?"

"Riana Thomas?" DI Holmes asked.

"She works in a sandwich bar in a shop on Shepherd's Bush Green. She makes the local kids their breakfast before they go to school. She has to be there for eight on mornings."

"When does she get home?" May asked.

"About one-thirty."

"Okay," said Holmes.

"What money do you think they were referring to?" DI May asked.

"You asking me?" Tom asked.

"Yeah. I'm asking you," May said with an attitude in his tone.

"No idea. If the guy I took to the hospital had some cash on him I never saw it."

DI May sniffed as if he was trying to smell the bullshit coming out of his mouth. "So, you've got no idea what became of some money?"

"Me. No. None at all. Why should I?"

"Okay," said DI Holmes once again. "Another reason we're here is to show you some photographs taken from several CCTV cameras close to the hospital."

"Oh right."

"There are also some taken along a stretch of the M40. Perhaps you might be able to recognise a vehicle of interest to us. Take a seat."

Tom sat on the edge of the sofa. DI Holmes remained standing. DI May looked around the room, taking in the decoration and all the worthless trinkets. He stepped up to the metal frame photograph of Bob Marley above the open fireplace and examined some writing at the bottom of the frame.

DI Holmes opened the manila envelope and extracted several A4 size photographs. They were the type of image that could be taken from roadside cameras. There must have been a dozen of them. The Thames Valley police must have scrawled through hours of tape to find evidence of the movement of suspicious cars then taken still photographs from the film.

Holmes remained standing over Tom. "We need you to take a look at these."

"Fine," Tom replied.

Holmes passed the first one to him. It was a rather blurry photograph of a car, but it was obvious to see it was the Mercedes C200 he had been driving on that Tuesday night. In the top left-hand corner was the date in US format and the time in a twenty-four-hour digital format. At the bottom, right hand side was the location of the camera.

The time was 18:28, the date was: 02/09/16. The location was the A44, then a code which meant nothing to Tom.

Holmes cleared his throat. "That's your car travelling south along the A44 at twenty-eight minutes past six on that Tuesday evening."

"I must have been a couple of miles from the lay-by," Tom said.

Holmes passed him the second photograph. "Here's your car approaching Yanton. The time is now five to seven."

DI May turned back and took a step forward. "So, you've slipped out of the lay-by by this time and you've got the victim in your car," he said.

"Yeah. That's right."

"Now this one was taken in the hospital grounds," said Holmes. He passed Tom the third photograph. The words 'John Radcliffe Hospital' were embedded into the frame as a watermark. The photograph was clear. It showed the Mercedes driving along the internal road with the six-floor hospital building in the background.

"That's you, isn't it?" Holmes asked.

"Yeah. No doubt about it. I was on that road looking for the entrance to the Accident and Emergency unit."

"Now this one." He passed Tom the fourth photograph. This photograph showed several cars on the A44 at 19:26.

"You see that light coloured car? The five-door Vauxhall Astra." He leaned over Tom and pointed at one of the vehicles. It was a light coloured common model of car.

"We think that's the car parked in the lay-by at the time you drove onto it. It was taken less than one minute later."

It was DI May's turn to speak. "It's behind you. Its travelling in the same direction towards Oxford."

"Okay," Tom said.

"Compare it to the second photograph," DI May said. He placed photographs number two and four side by side. The camera place was the same location. Just the times were different by one minute.

"The white Astra saloon is following you. We calculate that he was about half a mile behind you. Did you notice the car following you?" May asked.

"No. Not at all. To be honest I was concentrating on driving through the wet. The truth is that the tyres on that car are as bald as a badger and I was having trouble keeping it on the road."

"Here's another photograph." Holmes passed the fifth one to him. "It was taken by the same camera as the third photograph. The one in the hospital grounds. It shows the Astra on the internal road going by the same spot."

Tom looked at it closely. "Yeah. Definitely."

"Now here's a series of photographs taken by cameras along the M40 going south towards the junction with the M25." He handed Tom photograph number six. "There's your vehicle just passing junction four."

This photograph was much sharper than those taken on the A44. It was a photograph showing the Mercedes C200 in the second lane with vehicles on either side. The time was 19:37.

"Now this one. It was the same place at 19:39. The White Astra passing the same position. They were following you into London."

"Looks like it. But they couldn't have followed me home."

"No, because they turned onto the M25, but you carried onto the A40 to drive into west London. They went south on the twenty-five. We can only assume they thought you had turned onto the twenty-five and they did likewise. They obviously lost you," DI Holmes explained.

"Geez. If they had stayed on the A40 instead of turning on to the twenty-five they would have caught up with me and followed me home."

"Yeah. But they were obviously near enough to take the registration. And that way they were able to find out Leroy is the registered keeper."

"Seems as if that's the likely outcome. What about the registration of the Astra? Have you traced that?" Tom asked.

DI May let out a strained chuckle. Holmes glanced at him momentarily, then continued. "These guys are professional criminals. It's what they do for a living. They use stolen vehicles for criminality. But we've had our eyes on them for some time. We know who they are."

"Oh my God. Who?" Tom asked.

"I'm not at liberty to say," DI Holmes said.

"So, what's it all about?"

"What?" DI May asked.

"The death of this Kemp chap."

"We're still working on the motive to that one. It's only been a few weeks since a raid on a Hatton Garden jewellery wholesaler netted the perps a lot of exquisite merchandise, worth about two million pounds," DI Holmes said.

"These two may have received some of the gear and were looking to move it up the chain."

"To Lyle Kemp?" Tom asked.

"That's the assumption we're working on."

"Oh my God," said Tom for the second time.

"Oh my God indeed," said DI May. "Which leads us to the question of the money."

"What money?"

"The money that Lyle Kemp must have had on him."

"I know nothing about that," Tom uttered.

"But he didn't have it on him when he entered the hospital."

"How do you know he had any money on him in the first place?" Tom asked.

That question seemed to faze both the DI's for a moment. Maybe they had not considered the possibility that Kemp had gone to make a deal, but never had any intention of paying for the knocked off merchandise.

"So why would they go to the trouble of breaking into your brother-in-law's place in Acton if they didn't think he had Kemp's money?" DI May asked.

"No idea. Have you considered the possibility that they are trying to con the people they took the items from? Perhaps they had no intention of paying them, so they came up with a story that the money had gone missing when in point of fact they have it."

DI Holmes looked at DI May. DI May sniffed again. Maybe this time he was smelling the coffee.

"Would you have any objection if we searched this place?" asked DI Holmes.

Tom pursed his lips then shrugged his shoulders. He retained a cool exterior, but inside his blood was boiling. "Be my guest," he said with an air of defiance in his voice.

Chapter 11

Within fifteen seconds of Tom saying the words 'be my guest'. DI Holmes was on a mobile phone communicating with a senior officer in the Met. He informed the person that Tom Scott had entered into a verbal agreement that his home could be searched, therefore there was no need to go to court for a judge to issue a search warrant.

DI May, then said it was purely procedure and that they had to carry out a search. Tom wanted to say 'whatever' but pinched himself, instead. Of course, he did realise that there was a good chance they would discover the money stuffed into the duvet on the top shelf in the airing cupboard. It was in truth, in plain sight. If they did find it what could they do to him? They couldn't take him outside and execute him on the spot. He would only get a couple of years behind bars for attempting to pervert the course of justice, or something like that. If he got a sympathetic judge on his side, he might spare him jail time. If he pleaded guilty at the first opportunity the leniency might even result in a reprimand and a suspended sentence. Prisons were full of hardened criminals with more waiting to join them. What would be the benefit to society of putting him, a chancer, behind bars? He looked at DI's Holmes and May and gave them no indication what-so-ever of the thoughts in his head.

Ten minutes passed, both the plain clothed detectives hadn't moved out of the sitting room. They obviously suspected that he had stashed the money somewhere in the house. Never mind all that bollocks about it being procedure, they seemed to have a good idea that he had it. There again maybe Tom was right. Maybe Lyle Kemp had gone into the wood with no money. Perhaps he did intend to steal the merchandise. Perhaps his killer had taken the money, but as Tom suggested they intended to double-cross their supplier. It was all ifs, buts and maybes. Still the villains had taken the trouble to break into Leroy's home and demand the money so maybe the police thought they were genuine. Everything would be settled if they found the cash in the house.

Fifteen minutes after DI Holmes had made the telephone call, a police van pulled up outside the house. The back doors opened, and half a dozen uniformed coppers got out. They entered the house where DI Holmes greeted them in the hallway. He issued the orders. Three were to search upstairs, including the loft. The others were to search downstairs including the back garden and the shed.

The search of the house began. Tom wondered what the next door neighbours would be making of it? That said, they were okay people who he chatted to now and again, and they tended to keep themselves to themselves, which was no bad thing.

The neighbours down the other end of the street were a different kettle of fish. The sight of a load of coppers entering the house would soon be the talk of Goldhawk Road. He prayed no one was preparing to go to the 'Salt and Pepper' sandwich shop to tell Riana that coppers where in the house. He also prayed that the police did not bring in a sniffer dog to sniff out the cash. Still he thought it would only be a matter of time before they found the forty-eight bundles of banknotes stuffed inside the duvet.

 The search began at ten to nine, by ten o'clock they still hadn't found the money. During the next hour, Tom stayed in the sitting room under the watchful eye of Messrs. Holmes and May. That said they did volunteer to make him a cup of coffee and raided the biscuit tin. All around him the officers were searching the house. Looking in all the nooks and crannies. He could hear them in the front bedroom, clattering about, opening drawers, and even moving the bed. By some miracle, and it was a miracle, they didn't think to remove the items in the airing cupboard. By mid-day they had failed to find the half a million pounds.

 The first realisation that they were on the verge of giving-up was when DI Holmes came into the room and asked him if he had a lock-up anywhere. He shook his head. Then Holmes asked him if he had a garage or any other storage premises in the vicinity. He shook his head for a second time.

 DI Holmes went out of the room and Tom stepped into the kitchen. Several officers were in the back garden looking for evidence of recently disturbed earth. A couple of them where in the shed looking through the gardening equipment he kept stored in there.

 One more hour passed. The time was getting on for one o'clock. At ten minutes past one DI Holmes came into the lounge. He forced a smile, but his body language said he was bemused and frustrated. He looked at Tom and gave him a face. Perhaps hoping that he would admit that he did have the money. Tom remained mute.

"I owe you an apology," he said, but he didn't mean it. It didn't sound sincere or genuine.

"Okay," said Tom. "Not a problem."

Holmes was going to say something else but decided not to. He had concluded that the money wasn't in the house, but maybe thought it was elsewhere.

Over the course of the next five minutes the officers left the house and climbed aboard the van parked outside. DI May had the good grace to wish Tom well and hoped that Leroy would pull through. Tom thanked him for his kind words. Then DI May and DI Holmes walked out of the front door. Tom closed the door behind them. He returned into the sitting room and looked out of the window. The two detectives were standing on the path at the end of his property to see the van containing the officers drive away.

Tom breathed out an enormous sigh of relief. He couldn't believe they had missed the duvet, but that's exactly what they had done. They must have discounted the possibility that someone would go to the trouble of unpicking the stitching to a duvet, create an opening then thread forty-eight wads of cash into the sponge, before sowing the hem closed. They hadn't even bothered to pull the duvet down from the top shelf. They assumed they would find the cash stuffed into a drawer or in a box at the bottom of a cupboard. Tom smiled to himself. He poured himself a vodka from the bottle he kept under the sink.

When Riana arrived home at one-thirty, after four hours of making sandwiches for the good people of Shepherd's Bush, Tom advised her to sit down. She thought he had some bad news for her. She looked at him, plaintively.

"What's wrong?" she asked.

"On the contrary," he replied. It was the first time he could ever recall using the word 'contrary'. He continued. "The police have been, searched the house for over two and half hours, but they failed to find the cash."

In a moment of relief, she laughed aloud.

"What are you laughing at?" he asked slightly annoyed by her reaction.

"The sheer madness," she replied. "Or the sheer incompetence of the Old Bill," she added.

"I reckon they'll be back with a warrant any time soon," he said.

"Why?"

"So, they can carry out another search."

"In that case, we'd better move the cash then," she said.

"To where?"

"Out of here. I've got the ideal place."

"Where?"

"The sandwich shop."

He thought about it for a moment. "Too tricky. They could be spying on us."

"Who?"

"Plod."

"You serious?" she asked.

"One hundred percent. We don't want to do anything out of the ordinary."

She thought about his response for a few moments then agreed with him and dropped the idea of moving the money into the sandwich shop. They briefly chatted about getting away for a couple of days, but again this was a non-starter. Also, they couldn't forget that Leroy was still in Intensive Care. If he remained there then they had to be close to home not only for him, but for Marie. Leaving London for a short break at this time would only pour unwanted attention on themselves. It would be an incredibly stupid thing to do in the circumstances. DI Holmes and May would see right through it in an instant.

Riana said she was going to call the hospital to try to speak to Doctor Guppta for an update on Leroy's condition.

Before she could make that call the landline telephone rang. Tom took the call. He was surprised to hear DI Drake introduce herself. She told him that there had been two major developments overnight. Leroy's Mercedes C200 had been found burnt out on a piece of waste ground in Haringay, north London. The second piece of information was far more important. Thames Valley Police in conjunction with the Metropolitan Police were going public. At a joint news conference at three o'clock that afternoon, they were going to name two people they wanted to speak to regarding the murder of Lyle Kemp. They were forty-year-old, Brian Peter Handley, and fifty-eight-year-old Curtis McVeigh. Also, known as Curt.

They were well-known criminals from the Birmingham area who had links to people in the jewellery trade. Tom thanked her. He did wonder why DI Holmes and DI May had not told him this information. Then it dawned on him, they were waiting until after the search of his house before passing on the information to him. Maybe now they had concluded that he didn't have any money, or maybe they were playing a game with him. Hoping that he would drop his guard and lead them to the cash.

As soon as Tom put the telephone down Riana made a call to the hospital and asked to speak to Doctor Anna Guppta in the Intensive Care Unit. She was put through to the unit, but Doctor Guppta wasn't on duty at this time. Still she spoke to a senior nurse who told her there had been no change in her brother's condition, though she was hopeful he was on the mend. It was a case of not wishing to suggest that he was better, then suffering a major setback in his recovery.

There was a lull in relation to the Lyle Kemp murder. Tom heard nothing. This was the way he wanted it to stay for a while. He didn't want to hear from any of the police officers leading the case. Whether that be the kind and gracious DCI Goodall, DI Drake, or the more assertive DI Holmes and DI May.

When considering what was going on, Tom and Riana tried to relax as best as they could. Leroy was still on the critical list, but the indications coming from Marie were that he was getting better and that was great news. A weight was being lifted from around Tom's shoulders.

Then at three o'clock, on this a Thursday afternoon, Riana took a surprise call from Doctor Guppta. Leroy had been brought out of the induced coma one day earlier than planned. Whilst he was still very ill and very weak after several days in a coma he was alive, and the longer-term forecast for a complete recovery was positive.

Riana said she wanted to visit the hospital. Tom advised her to stay at home, but she was adamant that she wanted to see him. He relented, and they went to the hospital together.

On arriving at the hospital, they made their way to the main reception counter. There were many more people around at this time than there had been the other day. Riana asked if she could talk to Doctor Guppta for two minutes.

She was told that Doctor Guppta wasn't in the unit right now, but if she went to the unit entrance someone would be there to meet her. They made their way through the light filled corridor to the unit. A female nurse was standing by the double door, waiting for them.

The nurse explained that Leroy had regained consciousness in the past hour. He was breathing on his own. He was aware of his surroundings and understood everything that was being said to him. He knew that he had been attacked. On hearing this, Riana burst into tears, not out of fear, but joy. Leroy, her flesh, and blood was back in the world of the conscious. The nurse said he wasn't out of the woods just yet. If his condition continued to improve over the next twenty-four to thirty-six hours he would be transferred into a recuperation ward. Tom was now convinced more-than-ever that Leroy was going to be okay. Something told him that it was all going to end well. He hoped he was right.

After the visit to the hospital, they returned home to Shepherd's Bush. In the two hours they had been out they had missed two telephone calls. The callers had left messages on the answer phone. One message was from DI Drake of the Thames Valley police asking Tom to call her. The second message was from Tom's son, Josh. It was the first time Tom had heard from Josh since paying his court fine. It was good to hear his voice. Tom called him back immediately. They chatted for the next twenty minutes.

Josh said he had heard about the attack on Leroy. Knowing that he was his dad's best friend he wanted to know what had happened to him and how he was doing. Josh had just turned nineteen years of age. He said he now had a steady girlfriend. He was studying a degree level Business Studies course, at a college in Wood Green, north London. He still lived with his mum in nearby

East Finchley. He sounded well. He was doing his best to get his life in order. The drugs bust had taught him a valuable lesson and thankfully he had turned his back on getting too deeply involved in buying and selling grass. His father had no idea he was involved in the trade. Tom wanted to lay into him and give him a piece of his mind but didn't.

Josh said he had been at a crossroads in his life. Instead of turning left down a street towards a place called prison, he had turned in the right direction and backed away from the route that would inevitably lead him to a criminal record and a life on the edge. They agreed to meet in a couple of days in town for a few beers, some food, and a father and son chat. Though Tom didn't say that.

Tom was pleased. He was hopeful of rekindling a relationship with his son. The love child he had made with his first serious partner. A former girlfriend called June Lambert. Josh and he agreed on a place and a time to meet then the telephone chat ended, and they went their separate ways.

The second call Tom made was to DI Mel Drake in Oxford. It was back to the case. DI Drake gave him some news that pleased him but worried him at the same time. Brian Handley and Curtis McVeigh had been arrested by police in Birmingham, then taken to Oxford for questioning by Thames Valley detectives. Tom assumed it would only be a matter of time before they were charged with the murder of Lyle Kemp. This would also link them to the attack on Leroy. He thanked her for the information. She didn't have to give it to him, but she had.

When Riana arrived home from the late shift in the sandwich shop he didn't tell her anything about the calls he had just received from his son or the one from DI Drake. Her concerns were still very much with Leroy. Whilst he was out of the coma and had regained consciousness, he was still in hospital and there was no assurance that he wouldn't have a sudden relapse. Therefore, caution was still the name of the game.

Chapter 12

Friday 19ᵗʰ February

When they visited the hospital the next day - Friday - the change in venue was stark. Leroy was now out of the Intensive Care Unit and in a recuperation ward just down the corridor from the ICU. Gone were the machines and the claustrophobic feel of the cellular room. Leroy was in a ward along with nine other patients who were recovering from various ailments.

Leroy was in a bed behind a closed curtain. He had a TV screen over the bed. He eyed his sister and Tom as they came through the curtain. In a round glass bowl were a half-consumed bunch of grapes and a couple of tangerines. He was propped up by a pillow. He was wearing a hospital tunic. The turn of the bed sheets was lying across his stomach.

Marie was sitting in a chair by the side of the bed. Riana went to him, kissed him on the cheek and held his hand. His eyes looked tired and lacked their usual sparkle. His skin looked paler and far more leathery than normal.

"How are you feeling?" Tom asked him.

Leroy's lips moved, but the words didn't come out straight away. "…Like shit," he replied in a deep husky voice.

"You look great," said Tom.

"I don't feel it," he said, again in a husky voice.

He was having difficulty putting the words in his head into his mouth and passed his lips. The blow to his head had obviously affected his speech.

Marie could see the look of concern on Riana's voice. "Don't worry," she said. "He'll get this speech back in a day or two. It's the blow to his head."

Despite the minor speech impediment Tom was relieved to see him looking so good. It was a major change from earlier in the week. But he also felt responsible to a degree. It could easily have been him in that bed.

"What do the doctors say?" he asked.

Marie looked at him. "He's on the road to a place called recovery. But he's going to be groggy for a couple of days at least."

"Of course," said Riana. "It's only to be expected after what he's been through."

Tom said he was going to get a couple of chairs. He stepped out of the cubicle. Other visitors were sitting at the beds of their loved ones and the sounds of lively conversation filled the ward. He asked a nurse if he could get a couple of chairs. She pointed down a corridor. He picked up two metal chairs and brought them back and placed them down next to Leroy's bed.

They sat there for the next hour engaging in conversation and encouraging Leroy to open up and chat. They talked about numerous things, but not about the attack. That could wait for another day.

Marie said that the police wanted to chat to Leroy in a couple of days to take a statement. Tom let slip that Thames Valley police had arrested two men. He didn't want to get ahead of himself, but maybe these two would be charged with the murder of Lyle Kemp and GBH or ABH on Leroy. Marie asked for their names. He gave them to her. She said nothing and neither did Leroy who had little idea what he was talking about. He didn't ask him for an explanation.

After an hour, a bell rang, the visiting period ended, and the visitors were encouraged to leave. Riana and Tom said they would return the following day. The last thing that Tom said to Leroy was to pass on Josh's best wishes for a speedy recovery, though it was obvious to see that he was progressing well.

That evening Tom received a second call from DI Drake. The content of the conversation came with a bombshell, attached. Both, Brian Handley, and Curtis McVeigh had been released from police custody with no charges pending.

They had denied been anywhere near the lay-by on the A44 and anywhere near Acton in London. The police had no evidence to place them at either of those two locations so were forced to release them, pending further investigation. They had been in custody for less than the twenty-four hours permitted by the law. Tom was no legal expert but assumed that meant that charges were unlikely unless a file was sent to the Office of the Public Attorney. There was no indication that that was likely to happen. Consequently, they would be eliminated from police enquiries. He decided to hold fire on telling Marie of this development until he saw her the following day.

Saturday 20th February

The next day – Saturday – Leroy looked a lot better. His colouring had returned, and his speech had improved. The bunch of grapes in the bowel had all but gone. All that remained were the small puny ones and the empty stalks. He was drinking increasing amounts of squash and energy drinks.

Tom asked him if he recalled anything about the attack. Marie was a little put out by the question but didn't say anything in reply. Leroy said he could recall glimpses and brief recollections, but it was still very 'hazy'. He said he thought he recalled the sound of the glass in the patio doors been forced, then the sound of the intruders in the house. He got out of bed to see what was going on. He went down the staircase to the hallway. That was when the intruders appeared. One of them grabbed him around the neck and put him in a choke hold. Then he recalled something of major importance. He thought he had heard one of them call the other: Joel, Joe, or George.

Tom asked him to repeat that. He did. Then Marie spoke up and said she had also heard the name of Joe or George.

Riana asked them if the police had been to see them.

"No. Not yet," said Marie. If this was correct, that one of the men was called Joe or George, then the two men who had been released by the Thames Valley police couldn't have been the two who broke into their home.

Marie, Riana, and Tom left the hospital at the end of the visiting hour and made their way home. Marie dropped them off outside their home in Shepherd's Bush then went home to Acton.

Once home, Tom wondered whether he should contact DI Drake or DCI Goodall in Oxford to inform them that one of the invaders to Leroy's home was called Joe or George, not Brian or Curtis. He asked Riana for her opinion. After talking it over they decided to leave it for the time being. What they did discuss, long and hard, was the idea of moving the money to another safe location. Though the search of the house had taken place two days ago, it was possible that DI's Holmes and May would seek a search warrant for a second search. But maybe they had decided that the search had been conducted thoroughly enough to suggest that any money Kemp may have had on him wasn't in the house. Tom and Riana elected to leave the money where it was, until such a time when it was prudent to move it.

After a light meal, they settled down to watch TV, on this Saturday evening. The weekend was slipping away, and they hadn't done much. Riana was out of the room taking a bath. At a few minutes to nine the telephone rang. Though he didn't have a clue who would be calling at this time on a Saturday evening Tom answered the call. Maybe it was Josh. He picked up the phone, hoping it was his son calling him to confirm their meeting the following day.

"Who is it?" he asked.

The caller didn't reply. Tom thought he heard a sigh. He asked who was there for a second time. This time there was the sound of a click as the caller terminated the call and the line went dead.

It was one of two things, either a nuisance caller or something far more sinister. He put the phone down, then he immediately went around the house, checking the windows and the doors. There had been a couple of break-ins in the area about three months ago, but nothing he was aware of since. The burglars had apparently called the homes to check if anyone was at home. In the wake of the break-ins he had added some extra security to strengthen the back door by taking a panel off and filling the void with a thick pad of insulation foam. He had also fixed a security light over the back door, which was triggered by movement. He was confident that any potential burglar wouldn't gain access to the house with ease. Then he wondered if the caller wasn't a burglar, but the police. He did admit to himself that the silent call had put him on edge and left him feeling apprehensive.

Chapter 13

Sunday 21st February

The next day, Sunday, Tom met Josh in a pub in Earls Court at two in the afternoon. It was the first time he had seen him in six months for a social event. The last time he met him was in different circumstances. It was to give him five hundred pounds to pay for the court fine.

Josh looked better than he did six months ago. He was developing into a wholesome good-looking guy. He had shaved off the goatee beard he had grown, which Tom didn't like. He had also lost at least half a stone in weight and looked a lot slimmer in the face. Some of his mates had tried to persuade him to go up north to watch an Arsenal football game. He had managed to give them a body swerve and stay safe in London. He was maturing and finally acquiring a bit of common sense. His mates usually went to football to get drunk and to cause trouble. He was coming out of his rebellious teenage years that had led him astray once too often. He now had a decent haircut and now resembled an ordinary Joe. Tom thought he had been destined to spend some time behind bars, but it looked as if he was finally wising up.

The pub around them was busy with Sunday lunch-time drinkers and the atmosphere was nice and relaxed, though the juke-box was throbbing. Father and son sat in a corner and enjoyed a couple of pints of 'London pride'.

Josh said he was head over heels in love with a girl he had met at a college event. She was an aspiring catwalk model. Tom was impressed but hoped he didn't have his heart broken by her. Tom showed his dad a photograph of her. She looked like a stunner. Blonde, slim and long legged. Josh was punching way above his weight, but he wasn't a bad looking guy himself.

Josh asked his father what had happened to Leroy. Tom told him the full story of how he had been to the interview in Worcester and how he had used Leroy's car to travel there and back, and how that could have led to the break-in at Leroy's. He didn't tell him about the money. The story, both amazed and worried Josh.

Tom asked him how his mum was. He said she was okay. She had recently got a new job as a temporary secretary in an office in the City. She was doing okay for herself. Tom said great. He was pleased for her. He didn't ask Josh if she had a new guy in her life. It was nothing to do with him.

He was made-up for his son. It seemed as if he was coming out of a rough period in his young life. He seemed far more focused than he had been for some time.

Father and son enjoyed each other's company and parted after a couple of hours. He wanted to have a lasting relationship with his son. He wanted to know what he was doing, but not to the extent were he was permanently looking over his shoulder and cramping his style. Josh was a growing man with his own views on life. Tom would treat him like his dad had treated him. With compassion and understanding, but not overly protective or intrusive.

Visiting time in Ealing Hospital on a Sunday evening was seven until nine. Riana and Tom arrived there at a few minutes after seven. Riana had purchased a bag of assorted fruit, Tom had brought a men's interest magazine for Leroy to browse. He must have been really bored between visits, with nothing to do except ogle the pretty female nurses.

Riana and Tom entered the ward and made their way to Leroy's bedside. Low and behold Leroy was out of bed, sitting in an armchair by the side of the bed. He was dressed in a pair of pyjamas and a brown and mauve striped dressing gown Marie had brought him from home. The change in his appearance from the last time they saw him the previous day was as stark as it was remarkable. He was far more lucid and responsive than he had been. It seemed as if a fog had been lifted from around him. The swelling on his forehead had gone down. It was now just a minor bump. The bruises around his eyes had changed colour from a deep shade of red to a canary yellow colour.

"Oh, my God," said Tom when he saw him. "You look a great deal better."

"I feel it," he replied.

"He could be home by Tuesday," said Marie.

"They just want to keep me in here. In case I have a sudden relapse. Not likely,"
Leroy said.

"You'll do as you're told," said Marie.

121

"I think I know who the boss is here," said Riana.

"Rightly so," said Marie. "The nurses," she added.

If Leroy was released on Tuesday, he would be back home less than a week after been admitted in a critical condition. An amazing transformation. Leroy took a glass off the bedside table, which was full of blackcurrant cordial and took a good mouthful. He put the glass down on the side table.

"Have the police been to see you yet?" Tom asked.

"I should say so," said Marie.

"They came here at three this afternoon," said Leroy.

Marie blew out a long sigh. "Spent about an hour asking questions," she said.

"What did they want to know?" Riana asked.

"They wanted to know about the break-in. The time. What they said. What they did."

"Did you tell them you heard their names?"

"Yeah. That's the first thing I told them."

"Both names?" asked Riana.

"Yeah, George and Joe."

"When they asked for the money. What did you say?" Tom asked.

"Who?"

"George and Joe."

"What'd you think?" said Leroy. "I told them there was no money in here, except for about fifty quid in my pants. I told them they could have it. But they didn't seem too keen to believe that answer. They must have had it in their thick heads that I had a lot of cash."

"Did you tell the police all this?" Tom asked him.

"Of course, I did."

Tom decided to get off the topic of the money in case Leroy began to get suspicious. "When you told them the names what did the police say?"

"What like?" Leroy asked.

"Did they recognise the names?"

"If they did, they never said anything to me."

"How many were there?"

"How many who?"

"Police."

"Three."

"Did they give their names?"

"Yeah. DI Holmes, DI May and a female detective called Carter." He looked at Marie. "It was Carter, wasn't it?" She nodded her head.

"How long did they stay?" Riana asked.

"About an hour," replied Marie.

"What's next for you?" asked Tom looking at Leroy.

"Out of here. I hope. I want to go home. Get back to work and get back into the swing of things as soon as possible."

After a few seconds of silence Tom changed the subject and chatted to Leroy about the day's football results. The ladies chatted on their own about some reality TV programme.

Visiting ended at nine o'clock. Marie was the last to leave the ward. She took Riana and Tom home to Shepherd's Bush in her car, then she went home to an empty house. Riana had suggested she stay the night with them, but she said she wanted to get home and have a good night's sleep in her own bed, which was understandable.

Riana and Tom were back home for quarter to ten. Just as they were settling down to watch the late evening news the telephone rang. Tom answered the call. He said hello, but there was no answer.

"Hello," he said again. Again, no answer. "Who is it?" he asked. "Stop pissing about." Riana looked at him with a concerned look on her face. "Who the fuck is this?" he asked.

The caller hung up without saying a word. Tom replaced the receiver into the cradle.

"Who in God's name was that?" Riana asked.

"Don't know. It's the second silent call I've had in days."

"Do call-back," she suggested.

Tom hit the call back function, but the message told him that the caller couldn't be reached.

"Can't call back," he told Riana.

"Did the caller speak?"

"No."

"Who do you think it was?" she asked.

"I've on idea, but I think it's someone who wants to test us. It could be one of those who did Leroy over."

"Are you serious?" Riana asked.

"As a heart attack. Maybe someone knows we've got the money."

"How?" she asked.

"Not sure. Perhaps we've been observed going to the hospital with Marie and we've been followed home. Anyone at the hospital could have seen us coming and going."

"That's true," she said.

Tom looked at her. "I think we need to take some drastic action."

"Like what?" she asked.

"Getting the money out of this house," he replied.

"How?"

"By asking Marie to take it and hide it in her home."

"Are you serious?"

"Hear me out."

"I'm listening."

"If we persuade her to hide it for us, then it's out of here. We'll share it with them."

Riana thought about the idea for a few long moments. "If that's what you think," she said.

"I think it makes plenty of sense. Old Bill could come back at any time and rip the house apart looking for it. And next time they'll be bound to find it."

After a few moments silence she looked at him. "I think your right. How do they know to ring this number?"

"Who?"

"Those who attacked Leroy."

"The same way they found out who's the owner of the car...Contacts."

"I'll call Marie in the morning and invite her for lunch."

"Good idea," said Tom.

Chapter 14

Monday 22nd February

The following morning, Riana called Marie and invited her to join them for lunch. Marie accepted the invitation. She arrived at their home at just before one o'clock. The fragrant aroma of a joint of beef cooking in the oven had permeated throughout the house. It was the Sunday meal they should have had the previous day. So, why not have it today?

Tom wondered how Riana and he were going to raise the topic of the money. They agreed to wait until they had at least had the food before putting it to her about hiding the money in her home.

The lunch consisted of roast beef with roast potatoes and broccoli along with a plentiful supply of rich brown gravy. Tom had purchased a decent bottle of plonk to go with the food. By the time, they had consumed the meal all three of them were beginning to feel a little bit merry.

Marie told them that she was looking forward to Leroy returning home the following day. Doctor Guppta had told her Leroy would need to convalesce for a week at least, then he should be as good as gold. The doctor had suggested they go away for a couple of days at least. Marie said, 'fat chance'. Money was too tight. Following the theft of their car, a replacement vehicle was at the top of their wish-list.

This was the opportunity Tom required. They were sitting around the dining table, each nursing a glass containing the last drops of wine.

"We could buy a new car for you," said Tom.

Marie looked at him. "How?" she asked. Then she recalled that he had a decent redundancy cheque coming shortly. She assumed he was referring to that.

"You'll need all the money from your redundancy payment to tide you over until you find a new job," she advised.

"There's a dam sight lot more than that in the house," said Riana. Neither she or Tom could guess at what Marie's reaction would be. She looked at Riana and narrowed her eyes in a quizzical way. The flow of the strong red wine in her bloodstream seemed to have taken the edge off her thought processes. Her eyes were glassy, and her words were ever so slightly slurred.

"When you say a dam sight lot more than that. What do you mean?" she asked. It was at this point that Tom hoped that the police had not bugged the house. He doubted it but couldn't be one hundred percent sure. Too late. They would know it all by now.

"There's over half a million pounds in used banknotes upstairs," he said.

Marie's eyes widened. "You're kidding. Right?"

"No kidding. Not at all," said Riana.

"It's the money the burglars who came to your house were looking for," Tom said.

"What!" she exclaimed. "They said that we had their money and…"

"We've got it. Half a million pounds," said Tom. He glanced at Riana, not knowing what Marie's reaction would be. He was slightly fearful that she would blow her top.

"Half a million?" she said in a state of disbelieve, then sat back in the dining chair and nearly fell off. She had to grip the edge of the table to steady herself. "How?" she asked.

"We think that the man called Lyle Kemp, the guy who died, was carrying the money to buy jewels and gems that had been stolen from that raid on a Hatton Garden jeweller wholesaler," said Tom.

"What raid?"

"The one that was on all the news channels over Christmas," said Riana.

"I don't recall it."

"Take it from us. It happened," said Tom.

"What's the connection?" she asked.

"We think this Kemp may have been buying some or all of the stolen jewellery. For some unknown reason, they decided to conduct their business in a wooded area adjacent to a lay-by along the A44."

"Oh, my word," Marie said. "So, how did you end up with the money?" she asked.

Tom told her how he had heard the two gunshots as he waited on the path. Then saw a man emerge out of the shrubs and carrying a sports bag.

Marie took her glass and finished of the last remaining drops of wine. Riana decided to take up the story, like she was trying to emphasis that their decision to include her in their plans was a joint decision, which it certainly was.

"When Tom took him to the hospital he left him at the entrance to the A&E unit. Rather than go inside and face the police he swiftly left," she said.

"I didn't have any insurance to drive Leroy's Merc. I thought I'd get into deep shit with the police. So, I decided to leg it. I've only just come down from the ceiling after dealing with them over Josh's drugs bust. Anyway, I digress. I left him in the hands of the doctors and the nurses who would see him all right. I didn't think he'd pass away, but he did. It was only later that I realised he'd left a bag in the car."

"When we looked in it. We got the shock of our life," said Riana. "We stayed up half the night counting the banknotes. There where forty-odd wads of cash. It came to over five hundred and seventy thousand pounds."

Marie's mouth dropped open. "Oh, my God. Half a million pounds," she said in a gob smacked tone. Her Aussie accent was just about audible.

"Yeah. Half a million."

"But why are you telling me this?" Marie asked.

"We want to share it with you and Leroy," said Riana. "Two hundred and eighty-five thousand each."

"You'll be able to afford that apartment near Manny Beach…" said Tom.

"Manly Beach," she corrected.

"Live out the rest of your days back in Sydney with Leroy. Enjoying the sunshine. Out of the shit and grime of London," said Riana.

Marie didn't say anything for a few long moments. It looked as if she was thinking it through. After five seconds of thought, she looked at Tom, then at Riana. "Could we get away with it?" she asked.

Tom titled his head slightly to one side. "If we play it cute. Don't advertise it. Yes."

"We won't suddenly buy a Porsche 911 on a sandwich makers wage," Riana added.

"The police have already searched this place," said Tom.

"They didn't find it? Obviously not," Marie asked, answering her own question.

"No," Tom confirmed.

"We hid it inside a duvet and put that on the top shelf of the airing cupboard along with the other blankets and things. The cops didn't reach that high…" said Riana.

"Couldn't be arsed," Tom added.

"Maybe it's a sign," said Marie. She was into that hocus-pocus of star signs, fortune telling and astrology. Maybe it was something which was meant to happen. It was almost possible to see the reflection of a Manly Beach condominium in the sheen of her glassy eyes.

"You could pay off the mortgage on your house in Acton, put it on the market, sell it in a few weeks, buy a place in Manly and still have more than enough to live on," said Riana.

It was a strong case for agreeing to help them move the money. Marie had often talked about going home to Sydney. It was on her wish-list, but she didn't have the money to buy a place in beach side Sydney. If ever she had it would be close to Manly Beach. With a view across the harbour and the aqua-blue waters of the Pacific Ocean. Here was her opportunity to fulfill that dream. She took in what they were saying to her.

"What do you have in mind?" she asked.

"That we ask you if we can take the money to your place and store it there," said Riana. "The problem we have is that the police may shortly want to do a second search of the house."

Tom continued. "There's no evidence that any money was ever in Leroy's car in the first place. It certainly, wasn't in the car that the police examined in the lay-by. But we think the police have their suspicions that Kemp was carrying a large amount of money to do a deal of some sort with whoever shot him."

"If they come back with a search warrant they'll find it the second time," Riana said.

"Also, we've had a couple of those silent calls," Tom revealed.

"What?" Marie asked swiftly.

132

"You know. The telephone rings. You pick it up but there's no one there. Nuisance calls."

"Just a minute. We had a couple of them the night before the men broke into the house," said Marie.

Tom looked at Riana. "Could be a coincidence. I suppose," he said.

"It might not be," said Riana.

"What do I tell Leroy?" Marie asked.

"We don't think there's any need to tell him for a while. He needs to convalesce," said Riana.

"So, the question we have to ask you is are you able to hide the money in your house?" Tom asked.

"How?"

"We'll take the money out of the duvet."

"Why do that?" Marie asked. "Why not just give me the duvet? It could be like you're giving me an extra blanket or something."

Riana glanced at Tom. "Yeah. That makes sense," she said. "The burglars know you don't have it. The police know you don't have it. They wouldn't want to search your place, so they'll never suspect you."

"How much?" Marie asked.

"In the duvet?"

"Yes."

"We counted it. Five hundred and seventy-one thousand," said Tom.

Marie blew out a long tuneless whistle.

It was six o'clock when Marie drove home to Acton with Riana for company. Riana had placed the duvet into a large hessian type laundry bag under some paperback books and magazines. They were in the house in Acton twenty minutes later.

That evening Riana stayed with Marie. She slept in the guest room, under the duvet containing the half a million pounds in cash.

Chapter 15

Tuesday 23rd February

Leroy Panther was discharged from Ealing Hospital on Tuesday at two in the afternoon. The fact that he was home less than one week after been admitted to the hospital was nothing short of a miracle. It was testament to the skills and devotion of Dr. Anna Guppta and her team of doctors and nurses. Tom vowed never to knock the National Health Service, ever again.

Though Leroy was home the doctor advised him to rest for the next couple of weeks, at least, and to refrain from any strenuous activity such as playing sports or anything remotely physical.

Marie agreed to tell him nothing about the money in the house, until such a time when he would see the funny side of it, which wouldn't be any time soon. Both Riana and Tom said it was a wise decision.

Wednesday 24th February

The following morning at nine-fifteen Tom received a surprise telephone call from DI Drake in Oxford. She said she wanted to give him an update on the investigation. They had checked Lyle Kemp's home computer which contained a list of contacts and other information pertinent to the case. The names of Joe and George were the possible names of the people he was meeting in the lay-by. Though they were probably false names.

Brian Hanley and Curtis McVeigh had provided cast iron alibies for their whereabouts and movements on the night of Tuesday 9th of February. They had been ruled out, for the moment. But, as DI Drake stressed, it was only for the moment. Both alibies could have been established way before the event, indicating that they were false.

Tom was amazed when he realised that two weeks had passed since the visit to the lay-by with the police. None of the London based detectives had been in touch with him since the search of the house, six days ago. It was looking increasingly as if they had concluded that he didn't have the money, even if there had been any money in the first place.

Tom was sitting in the kitchen when the landline telephone rang. He answered it. It had been less than an hour since the call from DI Drake. He wondered if it was going to be another silent call. He looked at the clock above the fireplace. It was nine minutes to ten. Outside, through the thin net curtain at the window he could hardly make out the light in the leaden sky. Today was going to be one of those days when it hardly ever got light.

"Who is it?" he asked, anticipating that he wouldn't receive a response, but he did, and it was a call he hadn't been expecting. He could hear Josh's hesitant voice on the other end of the line. He instantly knew it was him. His next few words sent a shiver down the length of his spine.

"Dad. I'm in trouble," came his stumbling words.

"What? What kind of trouble?" Tom asked.

"Two men have me."

"What you mean? Have you?" his dad asked.

"I've been kidnapped by two men. They've told me they're holding me to ransom. They want money."

"What money?" Tom asked.

"The money they said…."

The phone must have been snatched out of Tom's hand, as a new voice came down the line. "The money you took from Lyle Kemp," said an unfamiliar, loud voice.

Then there was silence for ten seconds before Tom asked. "Who is this?"

"Never mind. Listen to me. Let me ask you a question. Do you want to see your son again?" the caller asked.

"What?"

"Do you want to see your son again?" the caller asked, raising his tone of voice from a normal level and pitch to high and impatient.

"Of course, I do," he replied.

"Then do as I say."

"I don't have any money."

"We think you do." Tom's hearing sense was stretched to the limit. He could hear every intake of breath, every inflection of tone, every sinew of movement. His brain quickly calculated that it was a north London accent.

"I don't," he insisted, but instantly knew it was the wrong thing to say but he waited for his response.

"Whatever," said the stranger.

"What do you want?" Tom asked.

"What's up with you? Don't you hear too good or summat? If we don't get it, we'll start hurting your boy," said the caller with menace.

"Please don't hurt him," Tom said with a hint of pleading in his tone.

"That's down to you. Play ball with us and he'll be okay. We'll feed him and keep him watered. If you don't play ball, we'll have to slap him around a bit," said the voice.

Tom heard the word 'we'll', indicating that more than one person was holding Josh. The man suddenly chuckled. His laughed rebounded and echoed as if he was in an open, echoey space.

"Please don't hurt him," Tom repeated. "He's got nothing to do with this," he added.

"With what?"

"You know."

"So, you've got the money?"

"Yeah, I've got it," Tom admitted.

"You need to give us what's ours. That's the first rule of the game."

"How do I contact you?"

"You don't. We'll contact you."

"Okay."

"Give me your mobile phone number."

Tom read out an eleven-digit number, beginning zero-seven. The caller read the number back to him. "Yeah. That's right. Put my son back on will you."

"Okay."

"Hi Tom." A moment passed.

"Dad. Just give them what they want," Josh said with stress, tension and fear in his voice. "They're threatening me with all sorts of things," he said. He was trying to sound pragmatic and in control of his emotions. Though it must have been a traumatic time for him. It was for his dad.

"I'll get it sorted out. Try not to worry."

"Who are they?" Josh asked.

"They're mixed up in that episode I told you about the other day. About the guy who got shot." He instantly regretted mentioning that someone had been shot. Too late. Josh didn't say anything.

"Do you know where you are?" Tom asked.

The caller must have had the call on loudspeaker, because the receiver was ripped out of Tom's hand and the kidnapper came back on.

"He's strapped to a chair in a room with no windows and not much fresh air. But he's okay for now. That will change if you don't give us what we want," he said in a menacing tone.

"What do I need to do?" Tom asked.

"Get the money. Put it in a sports bag. Do you know the main entrance to the Westfield Centre?"

"Yes. But which entrance? There's more than one."

"Shepherd's Bush tube station. You know it?" asked the man.

"Yeah. I know it."

"Now listen very carefully," he said. Tom didn't reply. "Be there outside the front door at seven tonight. I'll call you on your mobile and tell you what to do. Got that?"

"Yeah."

"And don't be a hero. Keep the Old Bill out of this. Your boy will be released as soon as we get the money. Understand?" he asked.

"Yeah, I understand. How can I trust you?" Tom asked.

"Trust me? How can I trust you?" asked the caller.

"You can."

"You do the right thing and it will all end okay."

There was a moment of silence, then the line went quiet.

"You still there?" asked Tom. The caller had terminated the conversation.

Tom could hardly believe the content of the call. Whoever the caller was he had his son. But how did they know Josh was his son? He didn't have a clue. Then he pondered on the question. Maybe the kidnappers had followed him to the pub and seen him with Josh, then they followed Josh to his mother's home in Finchley.

Later they must have returned to the house and snatched him off the street. But how did they know that he had the money? By process of elimination of course. They knew that Lyle Kemp didn't have it on him when he was admitted to the hospital. It had to be with the man who had taken him to the hospital. They must have known that Kemp was carrying a lot of money at the time, therefore the other man must have taken it. Who were these people? Tom asked himself. He didn't know. Had he just been talking to the man who had shot Lyle Kemp?

He sat in the armchair and tried to clear his mind and think. After a few minutes thinking time, he decided to call Riana. He had to tell her of this development. He called her on her mobile phone. After a few rings it went to voice mail. He asked her to call him back as soon as possible.

Chapter 16

Ten minutes passed before the landline telephone rang. It was Riana. She wanted to know what was so urgent.

"Listen carefully. Something bad has happened," he said.

She must have known by the tone of his voice that he was anxious and on the edge of a meltdown.

"Like what?" she asked.

"They've got Josh."

"Who's got Josh?" she asked.

"I've just had a telephone call from a guy who said he's got him."

"What do you mean? Got him?" she asked.

"He's been kidnapped."

"Did you speak to Josh?"

"Yes."

"How in God's name do they know where your son is?" she asked.

"The only thing I can think is that they followed me to the pub in Earls Court, then followed him home from there. It's the only explanation I can think of."

"Incredible," she said.

"I know."

She didn't reply for a few moments, as if she was consumed in deep thought. If she was thinking that his son was somehow in bed with those demanding the money she didn't say it, but maybe she was thinking along those lines. The other possibility was that the kidnappers had easy access to information relating to Tom Scott and his son. Not likely, but not out of the question either.

"Are they bluffing?" she asked.

"No. I don't think so," he replied.

"How did they know his movements?" she asked.

"No idea. But they seem to be pretty good at tracing car registration plates, so they could have access to information telling them where Josh lives."

"What are we going to do?"

"We don't have much of an option, but to deal with them. Give them what they want."

She didn't agree with him instantly, but neither did she disagree. Like him she was gutted that after longing to have money like this someone wanted to take it from them, but she was pragmatic at the same time. She knew they had to deal with the kidnappers to prevent a tragedy that would haunt them for the rest of their days.

"What did they say?" she asked.

"What'd mean?" he asked.

"How are you supposed to hand it over?"

"I've got to be outside of the Westfield Shopping centre tonight at seven o'clock."

"I'm coming home," she said. "I'll be there in ten minutes."

"Okay."

Riana arrived home within ten minutes of ending the telephone conversation. She looked hot and bothered. She said the morning in the 'Salt and Pepper' had been especially stressful as the local schoolkids had been a set of 'shits'. Then she received his call; and she felt much worse. But the dilemma facing them put her work worries into perspective.

Her first question was to ask him what he was going to do.

"I don't know," he replied. But he did. "I don't think there's a lot we can do."

"What? Give them the money?" she asked.

"Would that be a problem?" he asked.

She looked at him with a cool expression on her face. She didn't want a morality test thrown in her face. She didn't reply.

"We're talking about my son here," he said.

"I understand that."

"If we don't deal with them, they're liable to hurt him."

"Like they did with Leroy," she said.

"Exactly."

"Maybe there's another way," she said.

"Which is?"

"We contact the police. Tell them."

"Tell them what?" he asked.

"Tell them someone has kidnapped Josh."

"Tell them we've got the money?"

"Not necessarily," she said. "The police don't think you've got the money. There's no need to admit that we've got it."

"Let me get my head around this," he said. "I contact DI Holmes and tell him someone's got Josh and they want the money, but I don't have it?"

"Exactly," she said.

Tom thought about it.

"How come they seem to know you've got the money. Did you tell Josh?" she asked.

"No. Of course I didn't," he snapped.

"Only asking," she replied in a snap of her own.

"I guess they knew that Lyle Kemp had the money with him the night they met him in the lay-by. As it wasn't in his car and he didn't have it with him when he was admitted to the hospital then they must know we've got it."

"If you need to be outside of the Westfield at seven tonight, then you'd best decide what to do pretty quickly," she said.

"Let me call Holmes. I have his card. I'll see what he says, then we'll take it from there. Agreed?" he asked.

"Agreed," she said in a halfhearted reluctant tone.

He found the card DI Holmes had given him. He picked up the landline telephone. Despite been told not to contact the 'Old Bill' he tapped the digits into the number keypad.

DI Holmes answered the incoming call after five rings. It was the first-time Tom had heard his voice since he had been at the house looking for the dough.

"It's Tom Scott," he said.

"What can I do for you?" Holmes asked.

"They've got Josh," he said.

"Who's got Josh? Who's Josh?" Holmes asked.

"My son. Josh has been kidnapped."

"By whom?"

"Two men. They've snatched him off the street."

"When?"

"I don't know for sure. Last night or today I would think."

"How do you know?"

"I've just received a call from one of them."

"Okay. When exactly did you receive the call?"

"About fifteen minutes ago."

"And you've only decided to call me now?" Holmes asked.

"I needed to talk it over with Riana."

"Talk over what?"

"What to do."

Holmes sighed. "You've done the right thing calling me. What exactly did he say?"

"That they've got him."

"What do they want?"

"The money."

"What money?"

"The money I'm supposed to have."

"Do you know for certain that they've got your son?" Holmes asked.

"Yeah. They put him on. I heard his voice."

"What did he tell you?" Holmes asked.

"That he's been kidnapped by two men. Then one of them came on and began to issue orders."

"Did you recognise the voice? Is it anyone you know?"

"The caller? No. I didn't recognise his voice."

"What have you got to do to get Josh back?"

"Give him the money."

"When? Where? How?"

"Tonight."

"Where?"

"I've got to be outside of the main entrance to the Westfield shopping centre at seven o'clock."

"Tonight?"

"Yeah."

"Then what?

"I'll get a call to my mobile phone with instructions. Once they have the money they'll let him go."

"I suggest you go along with it. If you want your son back you've got to level with me."

"What do you mean?"

"You've got the money. Haven't you?" Holmes asked. Tom didn't reply. "Look. You need to meet me halfway on this. Your boy's life might be in danger. These guys are serious players who don't give a fuck who they harm. You don't want to have that on your conscience for the rest of your life, because you refused to fess-up to me. I'll ask you again. Have you got the money Lyle Kemp had with him?" he asked.

Tom took a deep breath. He looked at Riana whose face was bathed in concentration. "Yes. I know where the money is," he admitted.

"Good. You're on your way to getting your son back in one piece. Its…" he paused in mid-sentence as if he was looking at a clock … "Just after ten-twenty. We've got slightly less than nine hours to get something planned. Tell me everything this guy said to you."

Tom told him again. DI Holmes said he would call him back in ten minutes. If the kidnapper called again he was to say nothing. Other than he was willing to trade the money to get his son back alive.

Tom put the telephone down and looked at Riana. In his heart of hearts, he knew he had done the right thing. She didn't have to ask the question. She knew what he had told the detective. His face told her everything she needed to know.

"You've done the right thing," she admitted. "Your son's life is far more valuable than any amount of money."

He wanted to cry and felt moisture in his eyes. The dream had gone. The half a million pounds was as distant as the sun in the sky, but her words were worth more than a million pounds. More than a king's ransom.

He clenched his teeth for a moment. "Thanks," he said. "I'm so sorry it's come to this."

"We'll just have to buy another lottery ticket on Saturday," she said, then blew out a long sigh. "Let's just hope Josh is going to be okay."

"I hope so," said Tom. "I can't face the thought of losing him."

DI Holmes called back after eight minutes. He must have had a conversation with his superiors because he seemed keen to get the ball rolling.

"Where do you have the money?" he asked.

"Look. Before I tell you. I want your word that no one is going to be prosecuted..."

"I can't guarantee that," Holmes replied. "I'll do what I can to gloss over it with those upstairs. I'll see what I can do to ensure no one ends up in..." he nearly said jail, then changed it to... "court over this. Except for those who deserve to go."

"All right," said Tom.

"So where is it?"

"I took it to Leroy's and Marie's home in Acton. The house that was broken into. Leroy knows nothing about it. It's all been put into a duvet."

"A duvet?" Holmes asked with an incredulous tone in his voice.

"Yeah. A duvet."

"I'll go to the house to recover the money. I'll ensure that they aren't hounded over this. Do they know?"

"Marie does. Leroy doesn't."

"Thanks."

"Don't you go to the house."

"Why?"

"There's a chance the kidnappers will have eyes on you."

"Can I call my sister-in-law? Marie. To tell her someone is coming to collect the duvet and to give it to you with no questions asked."

"Yes. Call her. Tell her to give me the money. I'll be there in thirty minutes max."

"How will you find the kidnappers?" Tom asked.

"First thing is we'll put an electronic tracking device into a bag containing the money. Leave all that to us. There's something you must know about the money."

"What?"

"It's not real money. All the notes are dud. Counterfeit."

Tom was both flummoxed and stunned at the same time. He couldn't grasp what Holmes had just said. "What is?" he asked.

"All the money in the bag Lyle Kemp had with him. It's not genuine."

"You're kidding? Right?" he asked.

"No. I'm not kidding. I'm deadly serious. They are as valuable as the paper they're printed on. All the serial numbers are the same. Didn't you notice?" Holmes asked.

Tom was still in a stunned state of mind. He didn't reply immediately. It took him a few seconds to reply.

"No," he said.

"They are," said Holmes.

"How do you know?" Tom asked.

"Long story. I'll tell you this much. Lyle Kemp was working for the National Crime Agency to help us to trap Brian Handley and Curtis McVeigh. We gave him the money. It was a sting operation."

"Oh, my word," said Tom. "Did you know that we had the money all along?"

"Yeah. We had a good idea. We were waiting for them to come after you. We didn't think they'd go for your boy."

Tom was shocked. He was practically speechless. If what DI Holmes was telling him was true, then the money in the duvet was dud. The half a million pounds was worth, absolutely nothing.

"What happened in the wood by the lay-by?" Tom asked.

"We're still trying to piece it all together," Holmes admitted. "Let's get your son back safety then once we have the kidnappers we'll be able to fill in the gaps. Let's concentrate on getting him back. Agreed?" Holmes asked.

"Agreed," said Tom.

"Call Marie Slater. Tell her we're on our way to collect the cash."

"I'll do that."

"I'll speak to you as soon as we have the money," said DI Holmes, then he ended the call.

Tom told Riana what Holmes had told him. That the money was worthless. It took her a while to believe him, but she did after he had explained the background to her.

He asked Riana to contact Marie to tell her that DI Holmes and his colleagues were on their way to her home to collect the duvet. She was to give it to him. No questions asked. He would explain everything to her later. Riana agreed to make the call. With Leroy at home convalescing, it might be tricky for Marie to explain it away to him.

Riana made the call to Marie. She first asked her how Leroy was progressing. Okay she replied. He was still in bed sleeping. Riana said good, then she broke the news to her.

She told her the money in the duvet was worthless. Marie was at first suspicious, perhaps thinking that some skullduggery was taking place. Riana told her what DI Holmes had told Tom. The police had been working with the National Crime Agency and had given Lyle Kemp a lot of dud notes. It was part of a sting to catch Handley and McVeigh who they believed were handling stolen items from a robbery on a Hatton Garden wholesale jeweller over the Christmas period.

Marie agreed to give DI Holmes the duvet. In many respects, she didn't have much of a choice in the matter. It was bizarre to say the least. Riana didn't let on that the two men who had broken into her house, may be the same two men who had kidnapped Josh and were threatening to hurt him.

When Riana ended the call, she looked at Tom. She knew that Marie's dream of buying a place in Sydney were in tatters. Her dream had been snatched away from her before it had begun, which in hindsight was no bad thing.

Fifteen minutes passed before Marie called back to say that DI Holmes and a female colleague, a DI Tracy Pinder, had been to the house to collect the duvet. Luckily Leroy was still asleep, so he had no knowledge of what was going on.

Riana apologised to her. She cursed the day Tom had gone to that job interview in Worcester. Marie was more philosophical and pragmatic about the whole thing. She was pleased she hadn't began looking on-line for that dream pad in a Manly Beach condominium. She said she knew that people like Leroy and her were the kind of people who would never have a lot of money in their lives - no matter what. They were never going to be that lucky. But at least she still had Leroy and he was on the mend.

DI Holmes called Tom. He wanted him to wait until four o'clock that afternoon then sneak out of his house without been observed. He was to take a taxi to Paddington Green police station. A briefing would take place at half past the hour. DI Holmes and his colleagues were putting a plan of action together. The priorities were to - one, find Josh, and two, to apprehend those who had some of the stolen loot from the raid on the Hatton Garden wholesaler.

Chapter 17

Tom had no wish to upset the police, so he did as he was told. He waited at home until the clock hit four, then at that hour, he went into the back garden, climbed over a low wall, then walked along a cobble stone ally-way before coming out onto the street that ran parallel to the one he lived on. From there he walked the short distance onto Uxbridge Road to a mini cab office, near to the 'Salt and Pepper'. At a taxi office he took a cab to Paddington Green Police station.

It had been five or six years since he had walked into this place, then it had been to make a statement about a break in at the lorry depot he worked in in west London. At the time, a few businesses had been targeted over the previous few weeks by vandals. His depot was one of them. The CCTV had caught sight of one of the youths who had tried to set a lorry ablaze, luckily the CCTV helped to find the youths and put them away for a few years.

He stepped to the front desk and introduced himself to the female officer at the counter. He was asked to take a seat in the waiting area with several other people who all looked as glum as the dark skies overhead. All of them averted their eyes from his. The silence was tangible, other than the sounds coming from behind the doors that led into the inner sanctum of the station, which just happened to be one of the largest in central London.

A minute passed, then a telephone behind the counter rang. The uniformed officer answered the call, said a few words, then put the telephone down. She looked at Tom, beckoned him to the counter, pointed to a key pad secured door and asked him to wait there. He went to the door which was immediately opened from the other side by a burly looking male officer in uniform. The chap led him down a light filled corridor with doors leading into interview rooms on either side. The air was cool. There was no fragrance in the air.

At the bottom end of the corridor, Tom was shown into a windowless interview room. DI Barry Holmes, DI Phillip May and a plain clothed female officer were sitting around a table in the centre of the room. The wads of dud banknotes were piled on the table, four levels high. Now that Tom knew they were dud, they no longer had the look of beauty or the smell of value. The room had a plain tiled floor and the walls were dull battleship grey. The table was bolted to the floor. A pair of spot lights in the ceiling provided the illumination.

DI Holmes looked at Tom as he entered the room. He didn't smile at him, but neither did he frown or look pissed off. His eyes looked tired and he looked stressed with the trials and tribulations of police work at the sharp end of things. He gestured to a free seat at the table, then he introduced the lady to him as DI Pinder, no first name. Tom sat at the table.

DI Holmes cleared his throat. "You know everyone here. Let's make this quick. If they've got your son. You've got to play ball with us."

The door opened, and a fifth person entered the room. Another guy in plain clothes. Tom had clapped eyes on him before. He was an average looking guy in a sweatshirt and jeans. About six feet tall and well built. The most significant thing about him was that he was holding a black sports bag, that looked very much like the one Lyle Kemp had been carrying. The one that Tom had shoved into the charity metal container near to his local shops. The man came into the centre of the room and placed the bag down on the top of the table.

DI May set his beady eyes on Tom. "Look for yourself," he said. "All the serial numbers are the same."

"I'll take your word for it," he replied.

"No please check," DI May encouraged.

"Fine. If you want me to."

"We do…For the record."

Tom took a pile of banknotes and flicked through it and sure enough all the serial number of the tens were the same. It was the same with the wad of twenties and the fifties.

"All the same," he said. "I never noticed."

"That's because you never looked at them closely. No one ever does," said DI Holmes. "All they see is the cash. They were all produced by the treasury for police work. Do you think we would give anyone working for us work real money?" he asked as if such a notion was stupid.

"Who?"

"Lyle Kemp. He was working for us to track down all the stolen jewels from the raid on the Hatton Garden wholesaler. At the time you may have heard about it on the news."

Tom wondered if it was a question. He nodded his head. "Yeah, I recall seeing something about it."

DI Holmes smiled, then continued. "It would appear that those who met with him were trying to set him up to steal the money."

DI Holmes didn't have to tell him the full story, but he did. His voice echoed slightly against the walls of the room. The air was chilled. The atmosphere was frank and business like.

"We'll put the money into the bag. There's a tracking device sown into the lining. Hopefully, that will lead us straight to them and hopefully we'll find your son alive and well. A problem could emerge if they look at the notes closely and see that the serial numbers are all the same. Then they'll know it's a set-up. By that time, we hope to have located the place where they're holding your son."

"Hope?" exclaimed Tom under his breath. In that moment it came home to him that his son's life was on the line here. Anyone mad enough to snatch another human being and hold him to ransom must have been capable of doing anything. After all they had shot Kemp.

"Yeah, hope," said DI Holmes in a deadpan tone. "That's all we have going for us. We can't give a guarantee whatsoever that it will end well."

"Did they give you any idea where they may be holding him?" DI May asked.

"None," replied Tom.

"What about the caller. Did he give any idea of where he was from?"

"No."

His one-word answers didn't shine any light on those who had Josh.

"Tell us about the phone call, especially what you've got to do," asked DI Pinder.

Tom replayed the content of the conversation to them once again. That he had to be outside of the main entrance to Westfield shopping centre at seven o'clock that evening. In slightly more than two and a half hours from now. Once he was in position he would receive further instructions by a call to his phone. On a reasonably cool Wednesday evening, like today, the centre might be busy with shoppers seeking warmth and mall surfers doing what mall surfers do.

"Do everything they say," said DI Holmes. "Don't be a wise-guy. We'll have eyes on you from the second you reach the entrance. We'll have a team of six officers in the centre. We'll have an eye in the sky, watching your movements. And there's the tracking device in the bag."

DI May cleared his throat. "Just do as they say. Don't ask questions. If they tell you to do something. Do it. They may or may not frisk you. Don't resist."

DI Pinder took over. "The objective is to give them the bag with the money. The goal is to apprehend them, but also to find your son and free him. Got it?" she asked. Her tone was just as brusque as the men around her.

"Yes. I've got it," Tom replied.

Holmes took hold of the bag. "The device has battery life of twelve hours and a tracking radius of ten miles. It's the best we can do in the tight timeframe," he said in a defensive tone as if he wasn't sure it would work.

Tom nodded his head.

DI May and DI Carter then began to put the wads of banknotes into the sports bag. They didn't tell him where the tracking device was concealed, other than it was sown into the lining.

By the time the money was in the bag and the talking had ended it was getting on for six o'clock. The party left the interview room, took a left turn onto the corridor and out through a door and into a courtyard where a line of two unmarked cars were parked. There were several plain clothed officers in the first car. The light of the day was fading fast as the sun dipped in the sky. Tom's mobile phone was fully charged, courtesy of the police. He hadn't used it since he had called Riana this morning.

The cops got into the unmarked vehicles and made their way out onto the mean streets of London. Tom was in the second car with DI

Holmes and DI May. DI Pinder was driving. They followed the lead car and they headed south towards the rendezvous, through the stop-start traffic in this part of rush-hour London.

Chapter 18

The Westfield shopping centre wasn't just the largest shopping centre in west London, but the largest shopping and leisure complex in the whole of the south of England.

The kidnappers had chosen well. They had selected a busy location where plenty of people would be concentrated in a relatively small area and over a short period of time. The kidnappers had more chance to mingle in with the crowd and less chance of been spotted by CCTV or police surveillance. They also knew that Tom lived close to the venue. Today, the weather had been changeable. It had been overcast this morning, but then the sun had broken through the cloud and it became pleasantly mild towards the start of the early evening.

It was getting on for ten to seven when the unmarked police car containing Tom, arrived several hundred yards from the Shepherd's Bush entrance to the centre. The driver pulled into the kerb. DI Holmes told Tom to take the bag containing the money, get out and walk the short distance towards the glass-foyer entrance.

He got out of the car with the sports bag in his grip. DI Holmes's final instruction was to do exactly what they said. They didn't want a hero. They had it all under control. Not only where DI's Holmes, May, and Pinder on the job but they had requested the assistance of half a dozen other officers to be the eyes and the spotters. The centre's wide spread CCTV system would also be utilised to assist the operation.

Tom turned by the entrance to Shepherd's Bush tube station and walked along the paved walkway towards the centre entrance. Several people were around him. A bus on the service road to his left stopped at a terminus to offload several passengers. There was a hive of activity by the wide entrance with the overhanging canopy. He felt somewhat conspicuous with the bag in his hand. He glanced at his watch. The time was two minutes to seven. He checked his mobile phone to make sure it was turned on. Overhead the light in the sky was starting to fade. The walkway lights embedded in the path and those high on the centre façade were coming on.

In the next ten yards he was at the wide glass sliding doors leading inside the entrance foyer. The holdall was still tight in his grip. A wide assortment of people were coming and going. Just a few yards to his right was a rather stoutly built man in a dark security guard uniform. He was standing stationary on a spot. He had a communication device in his hand, which he was holding to his mouth. In these times of heightened security Tom must have stuck out like a beacon. The chap stopped and turned to look at him as if he suspected the bag contained something it shouldn't have.

He slotted the walkie-talkie into a knee-high pocket in his trousers, then he approached Tom in a measured walk. He was a white man, about five-ten tall and portly around the midriff. He had dark hair, possibly dyed and thick eyebrows. He wore black rimmed clear lens spectacles over his eyes.

Tom watched him come towards him. He was about to raise the bag and say it contained his work gear, but the man beat him to it.

"It's Tom Scott. Isn't it?" he coolly enquired, then immediately glanced around in a wide arch to take in the activity within his circle of vision. His eyes behind the glass lens were wide and he looked on edge and sweaty.

This sudden intervention not only stunned Tom but caught him off guard. He wondered who he was. "Yeah," he said in answer to the question. "Who are you?" he asked.

"Don't worry about that. I'm here to meet you," the man said. Once again, his eyes darted around the entrance. A group of five or six boisterous teenage girls were entering the centre, through the sliding glass door. Maybe he was a real security guard. He was acting like one. His body language was taut. He looked at Tom.

"Listen up. You need to go to the Primark store on the third level. Go to the men's section, select a pair of trousers to try on, then go into the changing room. Use the last cubicle on the left-hand side as you enter. Someone will be there to meet you. Got it?" he asked.

"Yes."

"Sure?"

"Yeah."

With that the chap turned away from him and calmly walked away from the centre at a leisurely pace. Tom turned the other way, stepped through the sliding doors, went into the inner concourse of the centre and approached a pair of escalators. One going up. The other coming down. The sights, the sounds and the smells enveloped around him. There was the beat of easy listening pop music playing over the public address.

He stepped to the information board in front of the escalators. He found the third level and the location of the Primark store. He recalled what DI Holmes had told him. 'Do exactly as they request'.

He took the escalator to the first floor, then up to the second and the next to the third level. The time was a minute after seven. He looked down the moving metal staircase. A single male was a few steps behind him. Was he one of the police officers? Or was he one of the kidnappers? Or just an ordinary member of the public? He had no way of knowing. A few steps behind the man were two young women laden with shopping bags.

Tom was soon on the third level floor. The floor space was lined with colourful ceramic pots containing plants and topiary trees. The glass and metal honeycomb roof above was gleaming. On this level, shopping mall musak was playing. Up ahead, about twenty yards across the floor was the entrance to the Primark store. He stepped around the big ceramic pots, across the open floor, ventured through the opening and onto the store. The shop was rammed with cloth racks. Walkways were set out in a gird which dissected the floor. There were few shoppers in the store. Staff in the shop apparel were standing chatting near to a pay desk.

Tom paused and stopped to look around to find the men's section. He couldn't get his bearings for a few moments. He went to a member of staff and asked her where the men's trousers where.

164

She pointed into the top right-hand corner. He thanked her then set off across the floor to weave in and out of the racks.

He was soon, amongst the sweatshirts, casual t-shirts, and the jeans. The bag in his hand seemed to have increased in weight. Perhaps it was the strain on his muscles. A sign attached to the partition wall said: 'Male changing room'. He went to a rail and picked a pair of khaki cargo pants off a hanger. He didn't check the waist size or the length. He had no intention of trying them on.

He stepped towards the entrance to the changing room. The pants were over his arm. The bag containing the banknotes stayed tight in his left-hand grip. There was a female member of staff standing by a podium just before the changing room. She eyed him as he came towards her.

"Can I try these on?" he asked.

"Certainly," she said. She saw the sports bag in his hand, but he looked kosher, so she didn't say anything. He entered the changing room and turned down a passage between curtained off cubicles on either sides. The curtain over the second cubicle on the left was drawn closed, but there was no sound coming from behind the curtain. He went passed the second cubicle, then he stepped into the third one on the left. Once inside he closed the curtain. There was a shelf at knee height against a back partition which had a mirror attached to it. He put the bag down on the shelf. He was half contemplating trying the shorts on.

Before he could undo his belt, the curtain came open and the face of a man appeared. He was a white guy, about his height. Slim in the body. He was wearing a black leather jacket zipped close to the throat. He wore a navy-blue baseball cap on his head with the peak pulled level with the arch of his dark eyes. He was carrying a hessian bag which had the motif of the Westfield centre stenciled across it.

"Tom?" he asked.

Tom felt a dryness in his throat. "Yeah," he managed to say before his throat seized.

"Put the contents of your bag into this." The man ordered and thrust the hessian bag at him.

"What?"

"Fuck sake! Empty the contents of the bag into there. Here, I'll help you."

Tom unzipped the sports bag. Between them they took the forty-eight wads of banknotes out of the bag and transferred them into the hessian bag. It took Tom a few moments to remember that the sports bag contained the tracking device. It was going to be of little use if he was using the hessian bag to carry the money.

He had no idea who the guy was. From what he had said his accent suggested he was local. Tom helped him put all the wads of cash into the hessian bag.

"When will my son be released?" he asked.

The man looked at him and squinted his eyes. "I don't know anything about that," he said.

"How much are they paying you?" Tom asked.

"Who?"

"The kidnappers."

The word 'kidnappers' seemed to irritate him. "I don't know what you're talking about. I was asked to meet you to put the content of your bag into this bag." He looked at the contents. "I didn't know it was full of money."

"By whom?"

"By whom? What?"

"Who hired you?"

"A man I met in a pub."

"Your joking. Right."

"Does it look like I'm joking," he stressed.

The man threw the final wads of cash into the hessian bag. Then suddenly from out of nowhere Tom's mobile phone rang. He took it out of his trouser pocket and looked at it. The man eyed him with suspicion. "Who's that?" he asked bluntly.

"No idea," Tom replied.

"Don't answer it," said the man.

"I have to."

The man turned away. The last Tom saw of him was him going out of the cubicle with the hessian bag containing the wads of money in his grip.

Tom answered the phone call. "Hello," he said.

"Where the hell are you?" asked the caller. His voice was full of rage. Tom recognised it as the same voice of the man he had spoken to that morning.

"I'm here."

"You're supposed to be outside of the entrance."

"I was."

"Don't fuck with me," he snapped.

"I'm not."

"So, where are you?"

"The guy in the entrance told me to come in here."

"Where?"

"The Primark store."

"Your making me fucking mad now. Don't do that," he snapped.

"But...but." It suddenly dawned on Tom that the chap who had just run out of the changing room may not have been one of the kidnappers. Tom made to get out of the room to follow him. Just then there was a hub-hub of sound as a group of four men entered the changing room. There was DI May and DI Holmes. The other two, two plain clothed officers, had hold of the man with the hessian bag and were forcibly pushing him back inside the changing room.

It was like a scene from some madcap movie with all six men pressed into a tight space. One of the police men said 'you're nicked' in the best tradition of TV cop shows. DI Holmes pushed himself to the front of the melee. He had a taut expression on his face. He opened the hessian bag and looked inside to see the piles of dud cash.

"Where's Josh Scott?" he asked the guy in the black leather jacket.

"He's not one of the kidnappers," said Tom.

Holmes expression changed. "What?" he asked.

"Said, he's working for someone he'd met in a pub."

Holmes looked dumfounded. He took hold of the guy by the shoulders. "Who are you working for?" he asked.

The man looked stunned. "A guy called Tony," he replied.

"Shit," said Holmes to no one in particular. A hush fell onto the area. Then there were one or two expletives and plenty of confused looks.

Holmes looked at Tom. "How do you know he's not one of the kidnappers?" he asked.

"Because the guy I spoke to earlier is on the phone asking me where I am."

"Which phone?"

"This one," said Tom and showed it to him.

Holmes looked confused. "Is he still on?" he enquired.

Tom put the telephone to his mouth. "Are you still there?" he asked. There was no response. "I think he's gone," Tom said.

"Where is here?" Holmes asked.

"Out front I'd guess. Where I was supposed to be."

"Quick. Put the money back in the bag," Holmes instructed his colleagues.

He and DI May took the hessian bag. Tipped it up and emptied the contents back into the sports bag with the tracking device in it. Then came the sound of someone's mobile phone ringing. Each of the cops checked their mobile devices. It was the mobile phone DI May was carrying. He asked his colleagues for 'ssshhhh' then took the call. He listened to the caller.

"Got it," he said, then he addressed his colleagues. "Curtis McVeigh has been spotted, leaving the centre in a hurry with another guy in a car."

"Have we got eyes on him?" asked DI Holmes.

"Yes."

"Tell them to maintain a visual. We're on our way."

He looked at the man who had come to get the cash. "Someone nap him. Take him to Paddington. As for the rest of us. Get into the cars and see where McVeigh leads us. He might lead us to the stolen gear."

DI May relayed the message to those in the car following Curtis McVeigh. He eyed Tom. "I suppose you'd better come with us," he said.

With that the four of them, three officers and Tom, went out of the changing room and back onto the shop floor. Several shoppers and staff were now standing around looking to see what was going on. It was as dramatic as it was chaotic.

Tom had a feeling it was all coming to a head. But the key question was: Would Josh be found safe? He didn't know. He could only hope.

Chapter 19

Within a few minutes of leaving the Primark store, the officers were stepping out of the centre and getting into the unmarked car parked along a service road, close to the main entrance. They were soon on the move and heading in a northerly direction along the A404, towards the Harlesden area.

The car following Curtis McVeigh and his accomplice was a mile or so further along the road. The occupants had eyes on his car, but little else. If they lost him now, they wouldn't be able to follow him unless they had CCTV assistance.

Tom was in the middle of the back-passenger seat between May and Holmes. He knew the roads and the area though the backdrop seemed to be changing almost on a weekly basis. It looked increasingly to him that they were heading into north-west London.

DI Holmes made a phone call to his colleagues and asked that extra men be assigned to the chase and that a tactical arms unit be placed on standby should a siege develop. That got Tom thinking that maybe this wouldn't end well. He felt his heart rate increase and the thud of his heart in his chest.

DI Holmes contacted the leading car over the radio. The officer in the leading car provided them with a running commentary on the location of the target vehicle. It had just turned off a stretch of road known as Duddon Hill and was now travelling southbound along the North Circular.

The car stayed on the North Circular for less than a mile, before taking a left onto a road that led towards Wembley Stadium. The area around the stadium was crammed with small industrial estates full of small to medium size units. The kind of places where, if the client paid the rent on time, then few questions were asked.

The following car was on the road that led up to the north end of the stadium. As the car carrying McVeigh neared the huge curved arch of the roof it turned off the road and along a thoroughfare that led onto an industrial estate.

The stadium soon came into view. In the patchy sunlight, the glass and steel structure was silhouetted against the dark clouds that formed the backdrop of the sky.

DI Holmes asked the following car to drop back so as not to alert those in the villain's car. The last thing they wanted was to have their cover blown. They had the registration number, the model and the colour of the car.

Tom remained tight-lipped. He was too tense to talk. After everything he had gone through over the past few weeks, he thought that the end game was in sight. If the police collared McVeigh and the other fellow, then hopefully they would soon locate Josh. But there was no way of knowing if that would be the case.

The following car reported that the vehicle carrying McVeigh had entered a small business park of no more than a dozen small units tightly arranged in a compact area. They were heading for a unit. Some contained offices, others storage units and several were just big enough to support a small manufacturing operation. As there were a proliferation of units then it was by no means certain that all were occupied.

DI Holmes suggested that the lead car wait until they were in place then they would drive onto the estate mob-handed and surprise those inside the unit. The last thing they needed was an armed siege.

The second car, containing Tom was on Central Way. About a minute or so behind the first vehicle. To reduce the possibility of being spotted the lead car had stopped short of turning onto the estate and came to a halt just before the turn-in.

In all there were nine police officers on the job. As the car, with Tom in it, came along Second Avenue, the driver slowed to allow the lead car to start up and take them through the gates and onto the estate.

Though the night was drawing in at a swift pace there was still some light in the sky. Ahead, there was a line of three brick constructed units in front of them, each with metal roller shutter doors. Various items, such as a couple of large rubbish skips were placed along the service road, with wooden pallets stacked up against one of the units.

Spotlights attached to the front of the units were shinning down to immerse the scene in a splash of illumination. There was a sign saying: 'To Let' attached to the front of a unit. On the other was a sign saying: 'Wembley Bathrooms and Plumbing'

There were no vehicles outside of the unit, except for the one Curtis McVeigh was in. The lead car drove up to the unit and pulled up parallel to the car which was close to the metal shutter. Graffiti was splayed over the grated metal surface. Above the shutter door there was a window. An inside light was on. It was only a small unit, perhaps for storage only.

As the two cars were in position all nine police men emerged from out of the two vehicles and moved towards the single access door. None of them looked as if they were armed. Though Tom had no way of knowing if that was the case. Maybe several of them were packing a firearm. If McVeigh and the other guy were armed, then it might develop into a Mexican standoff. The tactical firearms squad was still on its way to the location.

DI Holmes came forward. He felt the bonnet of the car. "Still warm," he declared. As he stepped to the door of the unit, the light inside went out. Those inside must have been aware of the arrival of the two cars.

DI Holmes rapped a fist on the metal door. The thud seemed to reverberate along the length of the three units. "Police," he shouted at the top of his voice; then, "open up."

Tom looked up to the now darkened window as the dark shape of a figure appeared behind the glass.

"Upstairs at the window," one of the cops shouted; then, "come out."

Oh my God, thought Tom. This was dramatic stuff. Just like in the movies. There was a sound from behind as a large Metropolitan police 4by4 vehicle appeared at the entrance to the estate. This must have been the armed unit. Behind that was a rather plush unmarked car with red and blue lights flashing in the grill.

DI Holmes and several other colleagues were now at the door.

"We know you're in there," one of them shouted. Then came a responding shout from inside the unit. The words were undecipherable to Tom. A cop shouted: "Curtis McVeigh. We know you're in there."

Twenty seconds passed with no other activity or shouts. Then there was a noise from inside as the metal door came open and a figure emerged out of the unit and came into the splash of illumination.

"We're coming out," he shouted. There was a second man behind him. As soon as they were outside they were surrounded by the plain clothed officers who soon had them on their knees and were clamping handcuffs around their wrists.

The rest of the cops went into the unit, someone found the light switch and turned the interior lights on. Tom wasn't asked to join them, but something told him to follow them inside.

Several the cops were standing close together, so they were in effect blocking Tom's view. They soon split, and Tom put his eyes on the incongruous sight of a figure with a hood over his head who was sitting, literally gaffer-taped, to a chair in the centre of the empty, concrete floor.

One of the police officers went to the figure, took the hood and whipped it off his shoulders. Tom clapped his eyes on his son.

Josh raised his head, blinked his eyes half a dozen times, then cringed against the bright spotlight in the roof.

Tom quickly went to him. "Thank God, you're alive," he said.

Josh looked remarkably unfazed by the whole episode. He looked remarkedly lucid and not that put out. Though that may come later. He had been held captive for several hours, even days and that was bound to stay with him for some time. The floor around him was littered with empty drink cans and a few empty pot-noddle containers. There were several metal containers here and there and several hemp sacks laid around them on the floor. Tom sniffed. He could smell the pungent aroma of stale urine.

"You okay?" he enquired.

"I'm okay," Josh replied.

Two of the police officers began to pick at the tape securing Josh to the chair. They soon had all of it off. Josh tried to get up onto his feet, but he was unsteady on his feet. He had to sit down again. He looked at his old man but didn't utter a word.

Three of the undercover cops were looking into the metal containers and removing a number of cloth sacks that had been used to conceal something deep inside the containers. The chatter suddenly increased in veracity as they found something of interest concealed inside one of the containers. They pulled out a Samsonite briefcase.

It was soon forced open to reveal an assortment of jewellery: gold bracelets and bangles, rings, lockets. It would appear that the officers had found some of the stolen loot from the raid on the Hatton Garden jeweller wholesaler.

During the course of the next couple of minutes several more plain clothed officers arrived on the scene. Curtis McVeigh and the other guy were put into one of the unmarked cars. A scene of crime team had just arrived, and they were setting up to take photographs and dust down the interior for prints and what-have-you.

Thankfully, a Hollywood siege had been averted. Josh Scott-Lambert was free. Despite feeling a little groggy and unsure on his feet he was fine. He was a young man. He would make a full recovery in a few days. The first thing he said he needed was a shower, a change of clothes, then something to eat, in that order. He turned down a police officer's suggestion that he go to a local hospital for a check-up.

DI Pinder volunteered to take both father and son home. She led them out of the unit and they got into the back of her car. She didn't say a lot and neither did Tom and Josh. They were fatigued from the experience they had just had to endure. Tom was just thankful to a higher body that his son had not come to any harm. Josh said he just wanted a shower and to sleep for a couple of days.

Twenty minutes after leaving the unit close to Wembley Stadium they were arriving outside of Tom's home in Shepherd's Bush. DI Pinder dropped them off outside. She said someone would be in touch with them the following day, when they would be invited to Paddington Green Police station for a chat, but it wouldn't be anything too 'arduous'.

Once home in his dad's place Josh called his mum to tell her he was safe. He cut the conversation short before she had the chance to question him to the third degree. Then he had a shower. Riana made them both a meal of omelette with salad, then the three of them settled around the kitchen table to chat.

Despite everything they had gone through it wasn't until one in the morning when they turned the lights out and retired to bed. It was now just a case of waiting to hear from the police to determine what if anything was going to transpire from here on in.

Chapter 20

Thursday 25th February

The following day, DI May called Tom, as promised, at precisely two o'clock in the afternoon. He introduced himself in his usual laconic way.

"Hi," replied Tom in an equally laconic manner.

"Can you and your son come into Paddington Green station, so we can interview the two of you. By the way how is he holding up?" he asked.

"Considering what he's been through he's holding up well," replied Tom.

"Make it for four o'clock today?" May asked. "We'll be expecting you," he added. He didn't give Tom a great deal of opportunity to say no, but he had no problem going to see the police. Whatever will be - will be, he thought to himself.

"We'll be there. What's to discuss?" Tom asked.

"We have to conduct interviews to clear up a few loose ends," May said.

"Do I need the services of someone with a legal background?" Tom asked.

"A solicitor?"

"Yeah."

"If you want to bring someone to hold your hand, that's down to you, but I wouldn't go to the expense."

From that exchange, Tom assumed he didn't have a lot to worry about. The police were not going to charge him with any crime. "We'll be there," he said.

DI May ended the call.

It was ten to four in the afternoon when both Tom and Josh entered Paddington Green police station through the front door and stepped to the reception desk. Tom introduced himself to a female PC at the counter. Within a couple of minutes both father and son were taken along a corridor by a uniformed officer and into the suite of interview rooms with the battleship grey walls. For some reason, he didn't explain why, the officer showed them into two separate rooms.

Tom was put into a smaller room than the one the previous day. There was a single opaque window high in the wall, so a wedge of natural light was cutting in through the gloom of the dimly lit space. On a table was a voice recording machine. He wondered if the interview was going to be taped. Perhaps he should have insisted that he had legal representation, after all.

He sat at one side of the table and waited for the two seats at the other side to be filled, by whom he didn't know. A couple of minutes passed. He was beginning to feel a little lonely when the door opened. Two men entered. DI Holmes was one. He didn't know the other fellow's name but recognised him as one of the officers who had been with them on the raid on the unit. He was a much bigger, older version of DI May. His hair was thinning, and his face was slightly more creased than his younger colleague. His hands were thick and his fingers short and stubby.

DI Holmes introduced him as DI Larry Oakes. It was a name Tom didn't recognise. Like DI Holmes he was wearing a light pastel shirt and a plain tie, the knot was down level to the second shirt button.

They were both carrying polyfoam cups containing a hot beverage. It was possible to smell the aroma of coffee above the neutral smell of nothing. They sat at the other side of the table but didn't turn the recording machine on.

DI Holmes adjusted his seat. He looked at Tom. "Let's make a start. Why don't you tell DI Oakes about how you came to be in the lay-by on the A44 that night?"

"I'm keen to hear the story from the horse's mouth," DI Oakes added. He retained a serious business-like persona.

Tom put his eyes on DI Holmes. "Am I under any kind of caution?" he asked.

"Leave it out," said Holmes. "This is just an interview to further establish the facts. You'll be on your way soon enough."

Tom sat forward in his seat, put his hands flat on the table and began to tell DI Oakes the story of how he happened to be in the lay-by on the evening of the 9th of February. He told him everything that had occurred from the moment he got out of the car to light a cigarette to the moment he left a dying Lyle Kemp at the entrance to the A&E unit at the John Radcliffe Hospital in Oxford.

DI Oakes didn't say a word. He maintained eye contact with Tom as if he was looking for a chink in his armour and the tell-tale sign of a lie. His body language remained open and his expressions were neutral. Tom concluded that he wouldn't be out of here any time soon. After five minutes of talking, without interruption, he had concluded telling them everything that had happened. Not just that night but an entire review of the events from the start to finish.

He ended by saying, "I've told you everything," then he glanced at his watch. "I've been in here for fifteen minutes," he said.

"We know. We've been listening to you," said DI Oakes.

"How about you tell me something," Tom asked.

Holmes narrowed his eyes. "Like what?"

"What the hell was all this about?" he asked.

Holmes tipped his head slightly to one side, then glanced out of the corner of his eye to his colleague. "Fair enough. I'll tell you because you were involved, but it goes no further than these four walls."

Holmes pondered for a few more moments as if he was debating in his own mind if telling a civilian was the right thing to do.

"We know that Brian Handley and Curtis McVeigh were involved in handling stolen merchandise from the Hatton Garden robbery. Then they tried to do each other up like a pair of kippers. They each wanted the money they thought Lyle Kemp had with him to buy stolen jewellery. They'd met with Kemp in Birmingham city centre about a week before to show him the stolen gear. They'd agreed on a price of £570,000 for the haul. Then they came up with a plot to double-cross him by taking the money but keeping the merchandise to sell to another buyer."

"No honour amongst thieves then," said Tom.

DI Holmes allowed himself a wry smile. "They agreed to conclude the business in a lay-by on the A44. Handley and McVeigh hired two brothers, the Mullins brothers, to be there to take the money from Kemp. One of them shot Kemp, but unbeknown to them Kemp was armed. The thing is Lyle Kemp had been working for us. He told us about the meeting in Birmingham and the planned swap that was due to take place in the lay-by."

"So, you knew all about it and gave him the counterfeit money?" Tom asked.

"That's right."

"Why?"

"Why what?" Holmes asked.

"Why was he working for you?"

"He just was. The reason isn't important. But it all went tits-up. The two brothers turned up and attempted to snatch the money."

Tom didn't want to question them about how if they knew all about the swap, they had failed to protect Kemp. Clearly something had gone very wrong. He changed his line of question.

"How did they know I had the money with me in the car?" he asked.

Holmes answered his question. "It was the Mullins brothers in the white Astra. They followed you to the hospital in Oxford, then onto the M40, but somehow lost you before you continued onto the A40. They turned onto the M25. The Mullins were able to trace the registration number of the car you were driving."

"So, they assumed the car was being driven by Leroy?"

"They traced it to an address in Acton and broke into the house, thinking that the money was likely to be there. Then they looked up his contacts and discovered you."

"Who are the Mullins brothers?" Tom asked.

"They're a pair of low-life slime balls from north London. Known to both Handley and McVeigh. This is where it gets tasty. Because this is where Handley and McVeigh began to doubt each other and begin to plot against one and another. Were a lot of money is involved they're bound to be conflicts of interest. They knew you must have had the money."

"I guess that's true."

"McVeigh suggested to Handley that the brothers kidnap your son. Handley agreed. He wants McVeigh to think he is working with him. But he is also plotting against him. They both come up with the plan to meet you in the shopping centre. But Handley wants to split the money with the Mullins brothers, so he can cut McVeigh out of the deal. His plan was for the brothers to intercept you at the front of the Westfield."

"So, this McVeigh had no idea that the brothers were now working solely for Handley?" Tom asked.

"That's right." Tom congratulated himself on keeping up with the plot. DI Holmes continued. "When you were at the front of the centre. We had eyes on you and observed Curtis McVeigh and another man entering the car park."

"He was expecting to meet me in the front of the centre," Tom asked.

"So, it seems," said Holmes.

"But he didn't know that the brothers were acting for Handley to cut him out of the deal."

"That's right. We followed you into the store. Once in the changing room we entered and nicked the other guy who was working for the Mullins. We also followed McVeigh out of the car park and followed him to the unit in Wembley. You know the rest."

"Was the guy who was dressed as the security guard also working for the brothers?" Tom asked.

"That's right. A rather cute disguise was that. We picked him up last night. We also arrested Brian Handley. We'll get Mullins brothers soon enough. Curtis McVeigh has fessed-up to everything and put Handley in the frame."

"For what?" Tom asked.

"Handling stolen goods from the Hatton Garden job," said DI Oakes.

"Geez," said Tom. He looked at DI Oakes, then back to DI Holmes. "What happens next?" he asked.

Holmes pursed his lips and looked thoughtful. "Handley and McVeigh have admitted their guilt but deny being involved in attacking Leroy Panther. The brothers deny killing Lyle Kemp. At this moment they're in custody and will be charged with something before the day is out. If they insist they didn't kill Lyle Kemp, they will go to trial sometime. That's when you'll be called."

"To do what?" Tom asked.

Oakes smiled. "To testify on behalf of the good guys. For your co-operation, any charges against you will be dropped."

Tom realised this was the quid-pro-quo. They had him in an awkward position. He knew it and knew they knew it. He didn't say a word or make a face. He glanced at his watch. He had been in here for a minute short of twenty-five.

"What happens to my son?" he asked.

"Nothing. We're taking his statement for the record. He should be done by now. He sure is a strong willed young guy," said DI Holmes.

Tom didn't think he was being patronising. "He takes after his mother," he said.

Holmes glanced at his wrist watch. "Okay, let's stop for the day," he said, then rose out of the chair, quickly followed by DI Oakes. Tom did likewise. The two detectives took him out of the room, down the corridor and back into the reception area.

Josh was seating in a seat, gazing at the smart phone in the palm of his hand. He looked cool in his dad's brown leather bomber jacket with fur on the collar. He clapped his eyes on his dad. He didn't smile. That wasn't his style. They stepped out of the police station together.

"Fancy a pint?" Tom asked.

"Why not."

They found the nearest watering hole, a pub along Edgeware Road. They had a pint of beer each and chatted about life, love and living in a mad cap city like London. After the drinks, they took a cab home to Shepherd's Bush.

Chapter 21

Tuesday 8th March 2016.

Exactly four weeks to the day after attending the interview in Worcester, Tom Scott received a letter in the post. It was from the Operations Manager of the firm who had rejected him for the job. The letter informed him that the successful candidate had left the firm after a week. They now wanted to offer the job to Tom. As a way of compensation for messing him about, they offered him an extra week leave and the use of a company car for six months. The salary was slightly less than the one he had lost when he was made redundant.

They asked Tom to call them at his earliest convenience to give them his decision. He called them immediately. He told the guy that he was pleased and flattered to be offered the job, but he was turning it down.

The reason? He was going to use his fifty-five thousand pounds redundancy cheque he received from his last employer and a generous bank loan to go into the sandwich making business. Riana and he were buying a seventy-five percent stake of the 'Salt and Pepper' from the current owner.

Riana and Tom were going to stay with making sandwiches but diversify by making and selling hot food, but also turn the premises into a café aimed at the local market, passing trade and football fans going to Queens Park Rangers football games at nearby Loftus Road.

Tom had had enough of the haulage business and Riana had had enough of working for someone else. She was going to be the manager. Tom was going to be her assistant. He had done the numbers. A business accountant had looked at the books and it seemed like a good thing, going forward.

As for all those involved in the A44 murder, Tom never did hear from DI's Holmes, May, Pinder, Carter, Drake, or the rest of the team. Brian Handley and Curtis McVeigh were convicted of conspiracy to handle stolen goods from the Hatton Garden job. They each received ten years in prison. The police never did capture those who did the job, though they must have had a good idea of who had committed the robbery. The Mullins brothers were charged alongside Handley and McVeigh for their part in the caper. They pleaded guilty to GBH on Leroy Panther for which they each received three years to run concurrently with the eight years they received for conspiracy to pervert the course of justice and for aiding and abetting McVeigh and Handley.

As for Leroy and Marie, they stayed living in Acton and remained good friends of Tom and Riana. Leroy never did know that the dud money had been hidden in his house. It was perhaps best not to mention it. He had received a compensation package from the state, worth twenty-five thousand pounds. Despite the initial worry he had come out of it financially okay.

Josh left the Further Education college with a 2:1 degree to pursue a career in Marketing. Months later he left that job to become an assistant to a fashion photographer he had met when he accompanied his girlfriend, Rochelle, to a fashion shoot. Overall, everything ended up as well as it could have. Tom and Riana were never prosecuted for hiding the money. Leroy recovered from his injury. Those who deserved to be put behind bars received their just reward.

If there was one good thing to come out of this, it was that father and son became closer. They had come through a difficult task without snapping under the pressure. As Tom's dad had often remarked. 'What doesn't kill you will only make you stronger.' Now Tom knew for sure what he meant.

He recapped on the premise about three bad things coming at once. Three good things can also happen at once. They had survived. Despite their wish-list not been fulfilled as they had wished. Life was going to be a whole lot better. That was their hope and their wish-list.

The End

About the author….

Neal Hardin lives in Hull, England. He is the author of several novels, novellas and short stories. His first published novel, 'The Go-To Guy' was published in March 2018, by Stairwell Books, based in York, England; and Norwalk, Connecticut, USA.

Before retiring in 2016, Neal worked in the Education sector for over 21 years. He enjoys travelling whenever possible. He has visited the United States and Canada on many occasions, along with Japan, China, Australia and other countries. He follows his local football team and enjoys most sports and working out in the gym. He continues to write and enjoys the discipline of writing and constructing great stories.

Neal Hardin is also the author of…
Dallas After Dark
A Gangland Tale
The Four Fables
Moscow Calling
On the Edge
A Titanic Story
The Taking of Flight 98
Perilous Traffic
Triple Intrigue
Soho Retro
A Trio of Tales

All these novels are available to purchase on Amazon
See me on Twitter @HardinNealp

Printed in Great Britain
by Amazon

19213531R00109